COMFORT ZONE

COMFORT ZONE

STORIES
GORDON E. SYMONS

MOONSTONE
PRESS

The title story, *Comfort Zone*, originally appeared in
Encounter Magazine published by *The London Free Press* where
it won second prize in the 1991 Short Story Contest.

Cover art: Madeleine Roske, *Jardin Lilium*, mixed
media (January 1992); by permission of the artist.
Cover art photography by R.J. Nephew.
Designed and produced by ECW *Type & Art*, Oakville.
Printed on Zephyr Antique laid, sewn into signatures,
and bound by The Porcupine's Quill, Erin, Ontario.

Moonstone Press gratefully acknowledges the ongoing support
of The Canada Council and the Ontario Arts Council.

CANADIAN CATALOGUING IN PUBLICATION DATA

Symons, Gordon E., 1930–
Comfort zone

(Southwestern Ontario fiction series ; 2)
ISBN 0-920259-42-1

I. Title. II. Series.

PS8587.Y56C6 1992   C813'.54   C92-093883-3
PR9199.3.S95C6 1992

Moonstone Press
175 Brock Street
Goderich, Ontario
Canada N7A 1R4

CONTENTS

CANE IN A RAINSTORM

Rain drummed on Will's umbrella like his mother's admonitions. The stink of automobile exhaust fumes pricked his nostrils. Depressed, he swivelled quickly up a side street, eager to flee noon-hour traffic, angry that a hurtling Honda had sprayed him with a six-foot wave of muddy water, disturbed that he had to spend his waking hours ducking, weaving and bobbing to avoid one disaster after another and seldom winning. An ancient stone church loomed ahead. Abandoned by its original congregation decades ago, the building now housed *The Church of Orderly Science*, as a modern, back-lit sign announced. Attached to the wrought iron fence was a stencilled placard that read:

TODAY
MYSTIC BAZAAR
Noon to 5 pm

Will scurried past the blackened-limestone building. A block away, still wondering what a mystic bazaar was, he spun around and retraced his steps. He collapsed his umbrella at the door and darted inside. Janet wouldn't approve. She abhorred anything religious, buildings included, and certainly wasn't likely to endorse people, places, or objects that qualified for inclusion in the "mystic" category. That was all the more reason to explore. In the cloakroom, Will abandoned his raincoat, rubbers and umbrella and followed a hand-painted set of arrows down to the church basement.

Curtained stalls outlined the perimeter of the room. A bank of tables split the area in two. Enthralled visitors huddled around the exhibits.

"Read your palm, sir?"

Will glanced to his left and saw an attractive woman behind a card table. She wore a purple paisley scarf on her head, wrapped gypsy style. Her eyes were bright, brown and penetrating. Janet would surely disapprove of her. His boss wouldn't be much impressed, either. But then, nothing impressed him, it seemed. After a 60-hour work-week, Will had spent the weekend rerunning spread sheets and rewriting the third-quarter report for this morning's meeting. The old man hadn't even said thank you.

Will plunked himself on a wooden chair and jabbed his right hand toward the palm reader as though punching an adversary. The young woman smiled, her lips a sensuous red. "That will be five dollars, sir." Will dug deftly for the money and pushed it across the table. The palm reader dropped the bill into a metal box and reached for his hand. "Let's have a look," she cooed. Her touch was cool and gentle. She looked like Marlee Matlin, and without wanting to he recalled the scene from *Children of a Lesser God* when the deaf actress emerged stark naked from the swimming pool. He still envied William Hurt.

"You have interesting lines," the palm reader said, softly. She stopped smiling, gazed down at his upturned hand. "You will have a long life, but I see you are less interested in how long life is than if love and happiness await." She looked up, saw affirmation in his eyes, and continued. "Your palm says you are a man for whom certain things are important. Let's see if I can get a more comprehensive reading." Her forefinger came down, feather-like, on the base of his hand, then followed a path that led to the bottom of his thumb and up across the palm below his fingers. It slithered back to the centre of his hand. Her finger curled in on itself and lay in his palm like a frightened hamster. The palm reader's eyes closed and Will heard her breathe, deeply and steadily.

He didn't believe in any of this; he had simply come to the mystic bazaar as a diversion. Palm reading, like wrestling, was pure entertainment. Wasn't it? The truth was he'd sat down because the girl was pretty. Marlee Matlin pretty. It was pleasant to admire a woman close up; without threats, put-downs or demands. A man doesn't get the chance to do that very often.

8

"We believe what we want to be true," Janet had once proclaimed. "People are so easily duped." She said "people" but she meant him.

The palm reader said, her sexy voice searching, "You are a man who requires respect. Your life-lines say it is important to be accepted. By bosses and coworkers. Some men shrug off what others think. Not you."

Will's boss had said, "This is not a very erudite report." He spoke as if Will weren't even in the boardroom, so there was no need to care about his feelings. "The numbers many not be bad, but frankly, gentlemen, I have a grandson who could write a better narrative than this." Will wished he'd been able to conjure up a brilliant rejoinder, had stood up to the old man, just this once.

The girl's finger uncoiled to explore again, so gently he barely felt it roam. "Let me look at your relationship line." The girl's hands, delicate yet powerful, were far more expressive than her words. Will forced from his mind the thought of her fingers roaming elsewhere over his body.

What she'd said was true, but there was nothing mystical about that. Motherhood. Apple pie. Still, he didn't mind. This was fun, and fun was what he'd paid for.

"I see a woman in your life: a fine woman. However, the relationship is not fulfilling. In fact, she treats you more like a child than a partner. Am I right?"

He sucked back his hand and scrambled to his feet. He didn't want to hear any more. "Thank you," he said, back-pedalling into the aisle. The palm reader had no special powers; he was sure of that. She'd seen his wedding ring. It took no gift to guess that a 40-year-old man's love life wasn't as exciting as it once had been. Honeymoons didn't last forever. For anyone. Will just didn't wish to be reminded. Not today. Not after what had happened at breakfast. His long fingers scraped the side of his head, brushing away the memory.

A matriarchal black woman sat behind a small desk at the end of the aisle. She was large. Will could see swollen ankles protruding from the bottom of the desk. He supposed her brilliant red dress was part of the act, chosen to symbolize something or other. He sidled close enough to read the sign on her desk: PSYCHIC. Beneath, in smaller letters, it said, *Member – the Spiritualist Association of Great Britain.*

Of all the things about Will which Janet didn't approve, his sudden desire to see a psychic would undoubtedly top the list. He stepped into the booth and saw, too late, the white cane that sprawled on the floor beside her chair. He wished she'd worn dark glasses so he couldn't see the slowly drifting eyeballs. He said, "Hello there. Are you available for a consultation?"

The psychic said nothing for a moment. She twisted her head, listened, sniffed as if she were the puppy he'd never been allowed to have, then held out a shiny plump hand until he grasped it. I am available. The fee is ten dollars." She accepted his money and stuffed it down the front of her red dress. "Do y'all have a watch?"

"Yes."

"Is it new?"

"No. I've had it for many years."

"Good. Will y'all hand it to me, please?"

Will removed his wristwatch and placed it in the psychic's waiting hand. A smell drifted across the table from her body. He found it strange, though not offensive. It was like burning incense; the smell of boyhood in a St. John's basilica, abandoned 30 years ago. He studied the woman's face. She must be at least sixty, he decided, and wondered if she'd been born blind or had lost her sight later. He'd read that blindness intensifies the remaining senses. This should be an interesting experience. He didn't believe in psychic phenomena any more than he believed in palm reading, but he did anticipate the diversion of the event.

The black woman said, "Your mamma didn't treat y'all no good." She held his watch against her huge bosom as though it were an ailing infant, and shook her head.

The statement startled Will. There was no way this blind woman with thick, swollen ankles could have known — or even guessed — at the relationship between him and his mother. He had not made an appointment in advance. She couldn't have had someone check his background. Anyway, he never talked about his childhood. Not even to Janet. No one else knew but his mother, and perhaps his father, but they were both dead. There was no explanation Will could think of except that the black woman really *was* a psychic, and that was an unsatisfactory interpretation. There were no such phenomena. He leaned forward, straining to hear every soft-spoken word as the psychic rubbed his watch between her fingers, toyed with it, pressed it again against her chest.

"Your mamma was a pretty lady, I see. She belonged to lots of them fine ladies' groups but she don't seem to have had no time for y'all. A nuisance is what children were to that woman; one of them necessary evils. I declare, that lady didn't 'prove of hardly anything her boy did. I hear her say the same thing over and over: 'What a stupid thing to do, William. I don't know why you don't have no sense.' Lordy, that mamma of yours didn't treat y'all no good, nohow."

Will sat stunned. He'd expected stock comments. Trivia. Entertainment. Not this. Perspiration soaked his blue cotton shirt.

"Oh my," the blind woman said. "Oh my."

"What?"

"I see the car crash that killed your mamma. And your daddy. Y'all have had a rough time in this here life, I can surely see that."

He didn't want to believe, but couldn't ignore such powerful evidence. What if it was true? What if his parents really were talking to the woman? He had to know more.

"Ma'am, can you *talk* to people in the past, as well as see them?"

The woman in the red dress said, "Not so much that I talk to 'em, as that they all talk to me. If'n they all wants to. They don't, always." She raised Will's watch to her temple, brushed it lightly past lips the colour of liver. Her head fell back and stayed that way for several minutes. Will had no idea what was happening. Was the woman in a trance? Should he speak? Was the consultation over? He had to get his watch back. Janet wouldn't believe what had happened. She'd be angry; insist he'd wasted their money. If he told her, that is, which he didn't intend to do. No way.

The psychic said, "Your mamma feels poorly about how she treated you." Her voice was low, a monotone. "Your daddy allows she didn't know how to behave around y'all. She's sorry now for that. She surely is. That's something your daddy wants y'all to know. He wants y'all to understand he did believe you were a truly fine child. Truly." The psychic's head slipped forward. Tipped left. Then she returned his watch.

Will shook his head. "Don't stop." He took out his wallet and fumbled for another bill. "I'll pay you to keep going. Please. It's important to me."

"Ain't nothing to keep going for. Thank y'all for coming by."

She closed her eyes. Will had been dismissed.

Disappointed and confused, he wandered by the remaining tables at the mystic bazaar. He saw signs advertising aura readings and out-of-body experiences. A wizened man offered dream interpretations. A raven-haired woman studied tarot cards. Near the exit stood a short girl promising to read tea leaves at her tall tea-stand. Will was unwilling to tarry, afraid of doing yet another stupid thing. Instead, he wanted to prove to his mother that he did have good sense, that she could finally approve of something he didn't do. He'd stepped off one cliff and managed to survive his curious fall. That was no reason to seek new heights.

A strange day, this. He'd gotten up from the breakfast table, sauntered over to Janet's chair, and without warning dropped his right hand down the inside of her nightgown. He'd never done that before and had no idea why he'd done it today. "Let's make love," he'd blurted, embarrassed, knowing immediately from the stiffening of her body that she wasn't interested.

"You spend the weekend hunched over that damn computer, kissing your boss's back end, grovelling for some kind of juvenile approval and a pass to the corporate fast track, and *now* you want to make love? Now? How stupid can one man be?"

He winced. How stupid indeed.

Will hustled up the steps to the cloakroom two at a time. He paused to catch his breath, then was startled to hear his mother's voice, low and hollow but with every bit as much strength as the child in him remembered.

"Don't you dare go outside without your raincoat and rubbers, William."

He shoved his chilled arms into the trench coat that had his name written on its label, and tied the belt. Tightly. It was while Will was bent down, stretching on his rubbers, that his mother's voice thundered, "And don't forget your rain shade, William. Open the door, push your umbrella outside and snap it open, then step under it. Do what I tell you, Son. Mother only wants what's best for you."

Will thrust the umbrella out the church door. He was groping for the button that would unfold his black tent when he smelled incense; the incense of the black psychic. "Hell no," he muttered, then lurched outside. The rain pummelled Will's face. Cool drops dribbled into his eyes and ears, dripped steadily off his pointed chin. He didn't mind at all when passersby stared at the crazy man with a still-folded umbrella. Will jammed his shoulders back and rammed his chin forward. An umbrella was a fine object to use as a cane in a rainstorm, he though. Just fine.

He began to formulate in his mind how to tell Janet about his visit to the mystic bazaar. The best way would be to tell the truth. Right after supper he'd say, "I heard from Mother today, dear."

HAMILTON ROAD

Many of us live some of our years on a Hamilton Road. I was raised in a two-storey frame house on Pringle Avenue, which is two blocks south of Hamilton Road in London, but that's close enough. My dad, a custodian for the Board of Education and a good man, painted some part of the house every summer so it always looked good. One year he did the front porch. I climbed the ladder and scraped paint from the porch eavestroughs while my sisters giggled and slopped paint on the railing rungs. Another year we did the living room and the kitchen. Mom said we ought to paint inside in the winter when it wasn't so darned hot — and I agreed with her — but Pop said paint odours were bad for people's health and windows and doors should be wide open. In those days, Pop's word was the final word.

My dad believed in the London Board of Education. It knew what was best, he told us about once a week, for buildings and for people. There was a time to scrub floors, a time to refinish desks and a time to clean windows. There was a time to sit and learn, and a time to get out and play. The Board's schedule was rigid, he explained, for the good of everyone. Our lives were rigid, too: Sunday morning church, Saturday morning shopping, weekdays housework for Mom and my sisters. Except for making meals and washing dishes, my father didn't believe any work should be done on Sundays; that was not the Board of Education way.

I was twelve before I found out from Red Malloy that residents in other parts of London thought Hamilton Road was a blue collar, working class district. When I was twelve, I didn't see anything wrong with either blue collars or working, but Red called the people on Commissioners Road stuck-up snots so often I came to envy them just as much as he did. Neither of us thought it was fair that the geography of birth should have the potential to destroy our lives.

My first serious crush was on a 15-year-old girl who lived right on Hamilton Road. Her name was Teresa. She had a Portuguese mother and father (a marvellous advantage, it seemed to me then) and she was the most beautiful girl I'd ever seen. She was also a great softball player and joke teller. I loved being with her because she made me feel glad to be alive. Problems of all kinds — school, home or heart — were forgotten when I was with her. I had no idea there might be anything wrong with Teresa until I overheard my parents arguing one night in the kitchen. Mom's voice was pitched high, the way it gets when she's upset.

"I told you this would happen."

"So what can *I* do?" my father asked.

"Move. The mortgage is paid off. We could have moved to Westmount or Stoneybrook years ago."

I heard my dad sigh. I knew his bushy black eyebrows were being lowered toward his big bent nose. "I'm not taking on any more debt. Not at this point in my life."

"The least you can do, then, is change churches. If we go to Metropolitan United, and make sure the boy attends Sunday School and Young People's every week, he'll meet a better class of girl. This Teresa person is an immigrant's daughter, and a Roman Catholic to boot!"

Having to give up Teresa made me miserable for a long time. What's more, I never did go out with a girl from Metropolitan United. Not that there weren't some great looking women there, but they all seemed too tall and white and willowy, and already had tall and handsome boyfriends who owned Mustangs or MGS. I was short and chunky and what you'd call olive-skinned. When I was 15, the only thing I drove was an ancient CCM bicycle. I didn't impress any girls with that thing.

By the time I got out of school — after graduating, without honours, from Beal Tech, I shuffled through a three-year community college marketing course — I'd had enough of Hamilton Road. My dad had arthritis by then and my mom's hair was the shade of a bleached flour sack. Mortar dripped from our chimney and the white clapboard had been transformed into an acid-rain grey. My oldest sister got married and moved to a new subdivision in Oakville. My youngest sister dated a guy with a Corvette. She'd met him at the Met so Mom was happy about that.

I found myself a job as a salesman at a big-label recording company in Toronto (I called on stores and hustled compact discs and cassettes) and rented a spiffy bachelor apartment on Bloor Street. It cost me a big chunk of change, but the place had gold-flecked paper on the walls, a deep-pile carpet, and even a brass chandelier with tiny lights that looked like candles. I bought a book case. At a used book store I picked up volumes I thought were impressive: Ulysses, Homer, a set of Shakespeare covered in imitation leather, an Ibsen and a Dostoevsky. As soon as my life settled down, I intended to read them all.

My first priority, though, was to study my boss, a 30-year-old hot-shot on the corporate fast track, and emulate him. I bought the same shade suit, the same style suspenders. I wore identical Italian shoes and super silk ties. His business buzz words dominated my vocabulary and whenever I was in the office I made a supreme effort to swagger past the steno pool with as much of his elan as I could manage. It was tough to be exactly like him though, because he was tall and blond; I was still short. I did work out and lost some of my chunkiness and bought a pair of Italian elevator shoes. That was as close as I could get to becoming a cool, easy-to-love, modern man.

My boss gave me much good advice, like how pointless it was to date secretaries or record store clerks. His own attention focused on senior accountants, a junior lawyer and the advertising manager. I'd been with the company just over a year when, with my boss's approval and help, I created a strategic marketing plan to sell myself to our personnel manager. Might as well shoot for the best stuff, he said, and I had to agree.

Her name was Patricia Jane Rogers and she was just coming off a busted relationship, a terrific time to jump on a babe, my mentor told me. Patricia Jane was pleasant. She wore expensive suits and had a short haircut created especially for her by a Spanish salon in Yorkville.

Everyone said she would soon become a vice president, the youngest ever in our corporation (at least on this side of the border, though I didn't know what was at the head office in L.A.), and the first female. Patricia Jane had an MBA from the University of Western Ontario. I didn't tell her I had only graduated from Fanshawe Community College with a marketing diploma. I mentioned Yale a few times in casual conversation; it was a name I'd put on my job application and I guess she never got around to checking it out. She informed me the word "personnel" was obsolete, an insult to professionals in the field; "human resources" was the proper terminology now. Mostly I kept our conversations centred on her, the way my boss suggested. His theory was that women are happiest — and therefore easiest to control — when they're talking about themselves. I could not argue otherwise.

A lot happened that first year after I left home: my father had a stroke and died; my youngest sister, who got pregnant by the Corvette guy, married him at city hall, breaking our mother's heart because she never had a grand wedding herself and had been counting on the pomp of this one; Mom sold the house after that and moved in with an aunt in Chatham. So, one way or another, we all managed to get away from Hamilton Road. Nobody ever mentioned it, not in so many words, but I think the whole family was relieved that we'd finally grown out of — risen above, if you will — that lower-class London neighbourhood. I know I was pretty happy about it.

I leased some original acrylic paintings from a gallery on Bloor Street, gave away my CCR albums and invited Patricia Jane over. We'd known each other for a couple of months by then. She loved my taste in art, adored my collection of books and gave me the surprise of my life the next morning by volunteering to move in with me. My boss's advice had worked. Of course, I must have performed pretty well, too, considering how little experience I'd had until then. Life was finally starting to treat me right, I thought, and I grinned an appreciative acceptance of her generous offer. I promised to help move Patricia Jane and her belongings into my place the next weekend.

That room of hers remains in my mind to this day. It was a mere cubicle of a room on the third floor of a sooty brick house in the east end of Toronto. The walls were a dirty green and the wood floor was worn smooth. A bare light bulb hung from the end of a grimy brown cord. The hallways smelled of fried spice and other stuff I wasn't familiar with. I was glad Patricia Jane didn't have much to move except clothes and jewelry.

"I'm so glad to get away from this dreadful place, you know," she said, handing me a dozen blouses covered in dry cleaner's plastic. "East Indians live beneath me. Their cooking is gross. And Jamaicans live across the hall. Those are people who have loud parties; singing and dancing all night, you know, and only God knows what other kinds of carrying on. Down on the first floor there are Greeks and Ukrainians, if you can imagine."

"So why'd you move here in the first place?"

"Because it was inexpensive. I'd embarked on an investment program, mostly stocks and bonds, all blue ribbon, so I didn't have a lot of spare cash. One must get one's priorities right, don't you think? A little sacrifice now can guarantee wealth and security later on."

My life sure changed when Patricia Jane moved in. Mostly for the better. For example, I loved the way the women at work looked at me when they found out Patricia Jane and I lived together. In their eyes, I was suddenly somebody. It felt damn good, too, when the guys gave me the thumbs-up sign, which they did every day for the first week or two. There was no doubt I'd acquired a new, more important status.

I tried not to think much about how Patricia Jane was an inch taller in the high heels she wore from the moment she got out of bed in the morning until she stepped into the shower last thing every night. And though I was intimidated at first by the fact she was an intellectual, smarter by a ton, I discovered before long she wasn't any more sure of herself than I was. That was kind of a surprise.

"Do I look all right?" she'd ask in the morning, before we went to work.

"You're gorgeous."

"I don't know. I think this skirt makes my big stomach stick out."

"You don't have a big stomach."

"Maybe it's too short. My legs aren't good enough for a skirt like this."

"You have fantastic legs," I assured her. "It's a wonder *Playboy* hasn't asked you to pose. You're better looking than any of the women I've seen in there."

"If only I was a bit taller," she said, standing sideways as she looked at herself in the full-length mirror.

I told Patricia Jane that I loved her, and I believe I did, though I can't say — looking back on it now — that she inspired in me the same joy of life Teresa had once done. Of course, I'd only been a kid in those days. Things are different for adults, I guess. Patricia Jane and I didn't argue much. We split meal-making fifty-fifty. I'd have appreciated it if she'd offered to pay half the rent, but I didn't suggest it, knowing how she wanted to give that investment program of hers "a real kick-in-the-butt." Anyway, supplying shelter seemed the right thing to do for a man. She didn't declare her love for me, no matter how many times I told her, "I love you," but I was mature enough to understand that showing is more important than telling, especially when she snuggled up to my back in bed. The fact she'd moved in with me, I told myself repeatedly, was all the evidence I needed that I was, indeed, loved. There were more good times than bad, I'm glad to say.

Patricia Jane loved to talk about employment equity and the ramifications of a constructive dismissal charge. I learned a lot about human resources in the year we were together. I mention this only so you won't think our relationship was a total waste of time. She also taught me how to handle myself at executive cocktail parties. When we had supper with one of the vice presidents, she made sure I understood, well in advance, which forks and spoons to use.

"It's important to be seen as one of good breeding, you know," she explained. "The right background is essential for those of us who want to get ahead."

"The upwardly mobile?"

"Exactly."

Patricia Jane instructed me on how to dress for certain occasions, how to make introductions, how to tell a joke in mixed company and even the proper way to sneeze. She provided detailed instructions in the bedroom, too. Sometimes I wondered where she'd learned so much. She didn't explain, however, how to cope with her sudden departure from my Bloor Street apartment the day before the big announcement that the corporation was being restructured.

I was one of 25 people de-hired in a down-sizing project. I overheard one of the secretaries say Patricia Jane had moved in with the Vice President, Marketing, a slick fast-tracker everyone said was aiming for the president's office. He owned a luxury condo on Lake Ontario. Patricia Jane hadn't provided a single hint about the impending catastrophe and I was unable to make an appointment to see her in the damned personnel department before I was told to clean out my desk and leave the building. Can you imagine? A security guard accompanied me to the door. Patricia Jane never did return my phone calls.

I remained in Toronto as long as I could. My rent was $1800 a month, the payments on the BMW were another $1200, and incidentals like the cellular telephone and club memberships used up my severance pay quickly. Finally I returned to London, assuming it would be easier to get a job at 3M, or London Life, or maybe Canada Trust. Renting another fancy apartment was out of the question, so I checked out the "Rooms for Rent" section of *The London Free Press*. It was a shock to find a listing for our old house on Pringle Avenue. I drove out to have a look. Just out of curiosity, you understand.

Hamilton Road was about the same as I remembered it. A little better, perhaps. The Portuguese bakery run by Teresa's family had a modern new front. It looked great. I could still smell the bread as I drove by. Our house, however, had not been kept up. The paint had peeled off. The wood was dark and decaying. Porch rungs were broken or missing. A cracked window was patched with faded duct tape. A hand-lettered sign tacked on a now leafless elm said, *Rooms*.

I don't know why I knocked on the door. I was angry the house my dad loved so much had fallen apart, and I was also rather embarrassed to return, not glowing with the triumph of a successful son, but burdened with the shame of failure. Dad would have been disappointed, I think. His son had not scaled the corporate or social ladders. It almost seemed as though I'd never really left Hamilton Road. As I shifted my weight on the verandah from one Gucci loafer to the other, I was still just the common guy I'd always been. No improvement at all.

A round-shouldered man answered the door. The top of his head was shiny, though he didn't seem old enough yet to be bald. His green eyes were dull.

"Yes?" he said, not removing a pale, freckled hand from the door-knob. "Yes?"

"You have a room for rent?"

I shouldn't have asked. I certainly had no intention of moving back to this part of the city. This was no place to which anyone who thought much of himself would wish to return: not to the house I'd loathed as I scraped and painted it year after year; not to the house where I'd grown up feeling ashamed because I was only a janitor's son; not to a district populated mostly by immigrants. The man said, "I got one room left. Only one. Wanna see it?"

I nodded and followed him inside. Perhaps I hoped to see my mother still crocheting in the living room while my father sipped a beer and looked at *Popular Mechanics*. I missed her, suddenly, and him, too. And I longed to hear my sisters carrying on upstairs about who had last worn the pleated skirt or where the hell were the red pumps. A cockroach skittered beneath the fridge as we passed through the kitchen. I shuddered. Mother never tolerated any creeping creatures in her domain.

When we got to the top of the stairs the man said, "This is the room. Cool in summer, warm in winter. Quiet. Only 50 small dollars a week. In advance."

There was something familiar about the landlord. He was slick, glib, a used-car salesman with a sing-song spiel. But he was more than that. He displayed an easy sense of the self-confidence I'd always longed for but never could find. I'd been brash and cocky as a record salesman because my boss insisted that was the way you had to be if you wanted success, but it was phony. I was scared to death before every call.

It would be fine if I rented the room, this man's eyes said, but it didn't really make much difference to him, one way or the other. Take it or leave it. He was cool.

Then I recognized him. "Red? Red Malloy?"

He stopped showing me how large the closet was. His eyes narrowed. "You a cop?" He slithered back toward the door. "Ain't been no drugs in this place for more'n a year. Why don't you guys quit hassling me?"

Did I only imagine the fear in his voice? "I'm not a policeman," I said, following him out of the room, eager to ask a thousand questions. I also wanted to brag about Patricia Jane, my high-and-mighty modern woman, though I hadn't yet invented a credible enough reason for leaving her. I imagined suddenly that Red Malloy and I might still create a plan to get rich, to be accepted into all the best clubs, to have elegant women hankering for our companionship. Maybe it wasn't too late. All I said, though, before scurrying outside in the brilliant London sun was, "This is not what I'm looking for."

I didn't glance back until I had my hand on the door handle of the BMW. Malloy stood stoop-shouldered on the decrepit porch, a puzzled expression on his tired face. He didn't remember me. I wondered if he still hated the politicians and wealthy businessmen who lived on Commissioners Road. I slid behind the wheel. The BMW smelled great: real leather, rich carpeting, expensive lubricants. I knew when I turned the key it would burst to life and, just as it had transported me back to Hamilton Road, so it would spirit me away again. Forever, this time.

Malloy hobbled down the sidewalk. Then a smile of recognition brightened his face and made him look more like my old buddy. "I know you," he said when he reached the car. "You used to live in this house. We went to school together. We were best friends." He pushed his hand through the open car window and grinned.

My bones felt brittle. I needed to put the BMW into gear. That's what Patricia Jane Rogers would do, I was certain. It's what my old boss would advise. They'd both say that since there was nothing in this for me, no future at all, in fact it was a step backward, there was no reason to restart this relationship. I said, "Good to see you again, Red."

Malloy gripped my hand with a hungry kind of desperation and hung on. He babbled that my return to Hamilton Road had brought his own run of bad luck to an end. Finally, he said. Finally, for God's sake. Teresa's marriage had collapsed, he confided then, enticing me to stay. There were no children. Teresa was free. And just last week she'd asked about me. Still had the hots for me. Malloy said she was a terrific looker with bigger than ever hooters and I should give her a call. She'd love to see me. Really and truly, as God was his witness.

I wasn't tempted. Not even a little. She'd probably moved back in with her folks at the Portuguese bakery on Hamilton Road. It was important for a man to move up in life, to go forward, not backward. I'd learned a few things living with Patricia Jane. I disengaged myself from Malloy. Fired up the engine. Smiled. "Gotta go, Red. Got an appointment uptown."

"Give you a damn good deal on that room," Malloy said. "You don't even need to give me a security deposit." There was a pleading note in his voice. "I trust you, man. You know, just like the old days."

I let out the clutch and waved good-bye.

To Malloy.

To the decaying house.

But most of all, to Hamilton Road.

SOUNDS OF AN ORGASM

Carlin Black's Gucci watch told him it was only fifteen more minutes to Antigua. He looked forward to getting away from the couple across the aisle and their constant touching, snuggling, kissing and infantile giggling. More than four hours of it. Honeymooners.

Had he and Julia ever been like that?

Their honeymoon had ended so long ago he could hardly remember; it was long before he'd become president of the Skyway Cable Television Corporation. They'd been as much in love as these children, but they had not been touchers, had not been all over each other in public, not even in the beginning. They hadn't touched that much in private, either.

Of course, physical intimacy no more guarantees the existence of love than the absence of it proves love is absent. He still loved Julia. She said she still cared for him, too, but the separation had been her idea, not his. Unless this trip changed something — Carlin wasn't sure what — a divorce was certain.

The Boeing 767 reached for the runway gently, like Julia's final peck on the cheek. For a moment, he wasn't sure the tires had even touched the tarmac, but the shudder that surged through his body and the roar that hurt his ears confirmed the trip was over. Not for the honeymooners, though, who ignored the rapid deceleration with a wet, lingering kiss. Carlin looked away, imagining what they'd do later.

It had been zero degrees in Toronto. The Air Canada purser announced the temperature in Antigua was thirty. It felt more like forty as Carlin hustled through the humidity, angry that the plane had rolled to a stop so far from the terminal. The perspiration soaked his Brooks Brothers shirt and he prayed the building would be air conditioned. It was not, and since jumbo jets from American and Continental had dumped their passengers too, spilling them onto the broiling pavement like upended bags of brightly coloured marbles, the lines at customs and immigration rolled all the way back to the doors.

Carlin checked his Liat ticket to Montserrat. He had an hour before take off, plenty of time to answer inane questions, transfer his luggage, and pick up another boarding pass. Though the travel agent had suggested a later flight, he'd let her know he didn't plan to spend any more time than necessary twiddling his thumbs in a stupid tropical airport.

Once out of the 767, he left the honeymooners behind, not turning around to see what they might be doing now. The couples in the line ahead behaved themselves, acting as married people *should* act in a public place. He was grateful they were satisfied to look like tourists, unashamed of their straw hats, their Hawaiian shirts and skirts, and the simple point-and-shoot cameras that hung, like leis, around their pale necks.

Officially, he was going to Montserrat on business. To buy out the cable television franchise for the island, he'd told Julia. The imminent construction of several condominiums made the system viable. He'd already met with equipment suppliers, implied that Montserrat was merely the first system of a Skyway Caribbean Network: Guadeloupe, Dominica, Barbados. There were twenty-seven islands, he told equipment salesmen, bargaining prices down. Skyway had a professional purchasing agent but Carlin negotiated all but the routine contracts. He knew he was good at it; the suppliers hated him.

The Vue Pointe Hotel, north of Plymouth, was to be his temporary headquarters. An agent would show him a villa overlooking the ocean; only four hundred and fifty thousand U.S., if he liked it. Carlin understood it came with a maid, a grounds keeper and a cook. Skyway would pay for the villa, of course, and use it as an executive retreat when he wasn't there. Yet although this was one of Carlin's more interesting projects, it seemed unimportant: he'd really come to the Caribbean to save his marriage. He wondered why he'd been unable to explain to his wife.

The line inched forward more slowly than Julia's response to his frequent let's-make-love proposals. He calculated the distance to the desks, timed the next three feet of progress in the line, and determined it was impossible to make his flight without some string pulling. An airport official, a black man with gold braid on a crisp white shirt, stood off to one side, erect as a Buckingham Palace guard. Carlin coughed. The man paid no attention. Carlin didn't want to lose his place in line so he waved at the official.

"Excuse me."

Carlin said it again, louder.

"Excuse me!"

The man slowly swivelled on a polished black boot and glided away. Had he been a Skyway Cable employee, he'd have been fired immediately. Terminated. Ignore Carlin Black and suffer the consequences.

About a month after the separation, Julia suggested he get away for a while. To an island in the Caribbean, she'd proposed, smiling prettily over a cradled cup of coffee at the restaurant where they met to discuss support payments. She wanted him to go alone, to think things through, to sort himself out. There'd been a subtle but encouraging hint, implied in the texture of her flannel voice, that their relationship might be salvaged if he could find a way to separate himself from the corporation; get a divorce from the pressure, the stress, the ambition which — according to her — controlled his life. And find himself, she'd said.

"I have a friend who says the pace is a lot slower in the West Indies," Julia told him. "You haven't vacationed for years. Go, Carlin. It'll be good for your body, your mind and your heart."

He hadn't let her know he thought it was a dumb idea. He'd learned long ago not to be so honest. His standard reply was always, "I'll see." It was a political response that never got him into trouble the way the truth sometimes did. He wondered who the friend was. Man or woman? Perhaps Julia was already seeing someone else. Why hadn't she volunteered to come with him to Montserrat? Now that she was a partner in the law firm she could have arranged it. Couples had second honeymoons, didn't they?

The immigration official didn't look up as Carlin shoved his passport across the counter. Carlin made no effort to hide his irritation. "You made me miss the plane to Montserrat."

"Another one be comin', sir."

The man's black skin was smooth and shiny. The only evidence of age was steel wool hair gone grey, and a matching goatee.

Carlin said, "This is stupid. I'm not staying in Antigua; I'm just changing planes."

The official laboriously printed on the forms.

"I'll write the governor," Carlin said, fingers drumming on the counter. "This is disgraceful."

"Mention de badge number, sir: seventeen."

Julia had been attracted to him by his sense of urgency. She'd known from the beginning, when he was in his final year of engineering and she was just starting law, that he had a clear vision of where he wanted to go and was a man who didn't tolerate obstacles. She liked a man with goals. That's what she told him after revealing that her father was a free and easy drifter who'd never accomplished anything, had never been able to keep a job because of his drinking and the violence of his hair-trigger temper. Julia's mother had worked as a waitress to keep the family together; she had no intention of doing the same.

What Julia hadn't realized, or so she said when announcing the separation, was that Carlin had no idea who he was. "If *you* don't know, then *I* can't know," Julia explained, "and I can't live with a stranger."

Carlin was finally free to sprint to the luggage carousel, wrestle his Gucci bags to the floor, and nod to the porter who suddenly appeared by his side, a black genie with a red cap. "To the Liat counter," Carlin commanded.

He and Julia didn't fight often. Lawyers made him uncomfortable, always trying to trick people into saying something they didn't want to say. Lawyers take the position that one is guilty as charged. Their job is to make certain one doesn't get away with anything, even when one isn't trying to, and Julia was one of the best.

"Of course I know who I am," he'd protested. "And *you* know damn well who I am, too. What a crock!"

Julia had crossed her long legs, folded her evenly tanned arms, and said, "Tell me who you are, then."

He'd fled the condo. Immediately. Refused to participate in a discussion as childish as this. Had roared away in his Porsche, back to the Skyway office where there was always something to do, where people appreciated his talents. At Skyway he got respect.

Afraid his marriage was about to end, Carlin was surprised to find his anger tempered by a genuine sadness. But what could he have said if he'd stayed at the condo? His mother's reply to the question would be that he'd been created in the image of God. That's what she'd told him every time she criticized some youthful performance shortfall: an exam that earned him less than ninety percent, a school yard fight that bloodied his chin, getting caught shoplifting at Eaton's. His own answer would not have been couched in spiritual terms.

"I am Carlin Alexander Black," he'd probably have said. "An electrical engineer with an MBA from the University of Western Ontario; a husband. I'd have been a father, too, but you were too damn busy establishing yourself as a hot-shot lawyer."

To be fair, Julia *had* decided to take a year off to have a child. Her timing had been rotten. He'd only been a vice president then and the rumour mill had just predicted the imminent retirement of the president. Carlin had to work day and night, seven days a week, to make sure he beat out three other contenders for the job. He'd had some luck, finding out by accident about an impending hostile take-over. An offer to help the invaders from the inside — the group's leader was an old chum with whom he'd gone to university — allowed him to betray them at a crucial moment and save the corporation. Carlin became the youngest president in the company's history.

The Liat agent said, "Your plane left twenty minutes ago, Mr. Black. The next flight to Montserrat is filled, but I'll put you on standby. Check back in an hour."

"What do I do with these bags?"

"I can't take your luggage until I've confirmed the flight, sir."

"Well, I'm sure as hell not carting them around the damn airport." Carlin shoved a five dollar bill at the porter. "Leave the bags with him," he ordered, pointing to the clerk.

At the bar, he asked for a Chivas on the rocks. Five minutes later the honeymooners parked themselves at the table next to him and ordered Singapore Slings. They held hands. The woman, now facing Carlin, was pretty. As she gazed across the cigarette-scarred arborite at her husband, there was an adoration in her eyes that Carlin envied.

Steve Wurlitzer.

Carlin hadn't thought about him in years. They'd both been ten when Steve and his family moved next door. Mrs. Wurlitzer had accompanied Steve to the school yard, her plump arm draped around her son's shoulders. At the gate she embraced him, kissed him on the forehead and then gave him a departing pat on the behind. Everyone laughed, Carlin included, and after that they always called Steve, "Momma's boy."

Steve insisted he didn't like the attention. Carlin heard him say, every time he went to the Wurlitzer home, "Geez Mom, leave me alone, will ya?" But he said it in such a half-hearted way that his mother never did stop hugging and kissing him at every opportunity.

Then, Carlin had been embarrassed. Now, he was jealous. His own parents had been cool and reserved, not physically demonstrative, neither with each other nor with him and his sister. While growing up, that had seemed a blessing, but he hungered now for the lost intimacies of childhood. Because it was a stupid way to feel, he ordered another Chivas.

Less than two dozen passengers, the honeymooners included, jammed the commuter plane to capacity. From his seat, Carlin could see into the cockpit, a cramped cabin dominated by dials glowing green in a rapidly descending darkness. The pilot didn't bother to pull the curtain. Carlin saw his hand grip the throttles, jam them forward, and seconds later they were in the air.

One of the things that had surprised him about Julia was her reliance on horoscopes. They were the work of charlatans, constructed in such a broad way that something was sure to apply. *Keep an open mind, but do not be gullible. This is the time to display your sense of humour. Maintain good family relationships.* How could a woman of such intelligence believe in such trash? It was as stupid as his mother's blind acceptance of the Bible. There was no room for superstition in an age enriched by the triumph of science and technology.

To her credit, Julia hadn't tried to conceal her faith in astrology. On their first date — he remembered it was the day Princess Caroline of Monaco got married the first time — she'd told him what her horoscope said. "A stranger finds you appealing. Do not let your heart overrule your head." She also spoke freely of her belief in extra-sensory perception. At the time, he'd thought such talk was cute, an intriguing dimension of her unique personality, but the truth was he'd been so obsessed with the look of her — leggy and beautiful — that he wouldn't have stopped seeing Julia if she'd claimed to live in a space ship. He had to call the woman his own; had wanted her desperately.

Two immigration officers at the tiny Montserrat airport took less than five minutes to clear the new arrivals. At the far end of the room, however, a sullen customs man made every person open every suit-case, every shopping bag, every box. He pointed, without speaking, to the person he'd take next, motioning for the luggage to be placed on the counter and opened for inspection. The honeymooners were first. The bride blushed when the customs man held up crotchless panties.

The official bypassed Carlin, even though he was next in line, leaving him until everyone else was gone. There was no trouble, however. The man poked around shirts and shorts and an extra pair of Gucci loafers, then shrugged his shoulders and motioned Carlin on.

A group of taxi drivers at the curb, all black, huddled over a game of checkers. When Carlin dragged his suitcases through the door, a stoop-shouldered man eased himself away from the gathering.

"Mr. Black?"

"Yes."

"I'm Rainy Farrell, sir. I'm to take you to the Vue Pointe." He reached for the luggage.

Carlin checked his watch. He was more than three hours late.

"Were you here for the four o'clock flight?"

"I was, sir."

"And you've been here the whole time?"

"Yes, sir."

Julia had been right about the slower pace. No Toronto cab driver would wait and play checkers when he could be out hustling, making a dollar. Carlin supposed the driver would expect something extra for the delay; a large tip. Well, it wasn't Carlin's fault he was late. Ten percent would have to do.

The Montserrat roads were narrow. They twisted back and forth, climbed steeply, then plunged unexpectedly into the blackness. Goats, sleeping on the still-warm pavement, got up slowly under the glare of headlights. The driver refused to honk. Tethered cattle stood inches from the road, their round eyes drugged looking and reflecting the headlights of the taxi.

Julia had been an Annie Hall look-alike, hat and all, when they met in 1978. Adorable. She had few rules then. She'd go anywhere, anytime, did not expect to have money spent on her, had never insisted they go home early. She loved to walk: by Lake Ontario, through Yorkville, up Yonge Street. They spent Saturdays in High Park, strolling, sitting, talking. Movies were fun and they'd gone to many their first year. The only one Carlin remembered was *Foul Play* with Goldie Hawn and Chevy Chase, but he had no trouble remembering their eager groping in dark balconies, where Julia allowed herself to be hugged and kissed. She seemed to like the intimacy of it, had kissed him back with enthusiasm, but she permitted nothing more.

For the first few months, Carlin was happy enough. Challenges inspired him. He read the horoscope section of the newspaper and frequently tried to convince Julia the stars heralded that particular day as the time to consummate their love. Her interpretation of the message was always different. One night he blurted out, "Dammit, *when* then?"

Julia had smiled and run her fingers through his hair. "On our wedding night, of course."

Rainy Farrell tried to get a dialogue going, pointing out the house of the man who made the best goat water on the island, a hearty stew heavily laced with whiskey, offering to arrange a visit to George

Martin's *Air Studios* where the Beatles recorded all but one of their albums, and asking if Carlin liked steel band music. In the back seat, Carlin pretended to sleep. There apparently was no other way to keep the man quiet.

The Vue Pointe Hotel was a collection of six-sided cottages called rondavels, splattered on the side of a slope that fell gently to the ocean. Weary from his long trip, Carlin took little notice of the rattan furniture, the white-painted beams hugging the varnished mahogany ceiling, or the windows cut like horizontal Venetian blinds. The smell of palm and hibiscus accompanied the drape-rustling breeze. He stripped and crawled into bed.

The night wasn't silent as he'd expected. There was a steady squeaking, scraping, screeching: cicadas, bull frogs, night birds. Beneath those sounds was the rhythmic pounding of the surf on the beach below. He was just getting used to the background, had even wondered about having the sounds recorded and sold on compact disc because they had an exotic charm, when he heard the gasp of a woman, the grunt of her lover. He groaned. The honeymooners were in the rondavel next to his.

Julia had once been glad to give him such pleasure. What had happened? Could it be she'd never really loved him, had only seen security in him, a way to make it through law school? He tried to remember when it was she'd started being too tired; searched his mind for a turning point.

The woman next door moaned. The bull frogs quietened, as though not wanting to miss a single ecstatic breath.

Julia didn't seem to think that sex was important, except perhaps for young people, and then only to get a relationship off to a good start until deeper, better feelings were established. Sex was less necessary as a couple matures together, she'd told him once. She certainly did not appear to need physical intimacy any more. Not the way he did. But the problem was greater than just the loss of sex. Julia had stopped being Annie Hall. It wasn't just that she no longer looked like Diane Keaton. Her sophisticated new suits were acceptable enough. Some he actually liked. The tragedy was that she'd lost her playfulness, the girlish charm and easygoing attitude that had once so enthralled him.

The sounds of orgasm invaded his room. This was a stupid hotel. The rondavels should be sealed, sound-proofed and air conditioned. In fact, this whole trip was stupid. He saw that now. There was no economic justification for buying a Caribbean cable system; he'd made the journey hoping only to please Julia. If he went ahead with the sale, the shareholders would think he'd lost his ability to keep profits soaring. At the annual shareholders' meeting he'd said, "We don't call the corporation 'Skyway' for nothing." The *Globe and Mail* quoted him and the stock ran up two dollars.

It was also stupid to think a trip to this God-forsaken island could help a collapsed marriage. He should have told Julia that whatever it was she wanted him to think through could be thought through well enough in Toronto. Find himself? Carlin had no idea what that meant. He had no idea what he was supposed to look for, but he did know it wasn't necessary to be stranded on this piece of volcanic rock to conduct the search.

A mosquito whined in his ear, the final straw. He hurled himself out of bed, snapped the light on and chased the insect. How could anyone in his right mind operate a hotel without understanding the need for window screens? Not having them was stupid. Surely the owner knew that mosquitoes in the tropics were carriers of malaria, dengue fever — who knows what else?

A woman giggled. The honeymooners were at it again.

Carlin sighed. He couldn't go for a walk; he'd be eaten alive if he stepped outside. Even if the mosquitoes didn't get him in the dark, he'd probably step on an iguana or trip over a snake. He smashed the insect against the bathroom mirror and enjoyed his first smile of the day. A thorough search of the rondavel revealed no other enemies, so he crawled back into bed, more tired than ever, and yanked the sheet over his head to create an impromptu mosquito net. He'd complain to management in the morning. Better still, he'd cancel his meetings, charter a plane and get the hell back to civilization.

What would Julia say if he told her about all this? Probably what she'd already said, more than once. "Carlin, you're a perfectionist.

Everything in your life — and every one — must be absolutely perfect. Down to the last detail."

"That's the secret of success," he'd told her. "People aren't satisfied with products that fall apart, service that isn't, and relationships which meet no one's needs at all. In *my* company, if something goes wrong we have a man at your door to fix it within the hour. Customers expect perfection; that's what we give them."

"You don't expect your *customers* to be perfect," Julia snapped. "You allow for their quirks, their impatience, their lack of knowledge about certain things. It's the Skyway staff you expect to be perfect. And me."

The moaning next door grew louder again, the whines and grunts coming closer together. For the honeymooners, life was perfect. And why not? New love is blind; a man's imperfections are invisible. The bride was too busy to ask who her husband was. Unfortunately for the young man, her sight would return. Much too soon. Stupid questions would follow.

Had they finished? If not, Carlin vowed he'd head out into the darkness. The prospect of mosquitoes, iguanas and snakes was less ominous than having to endure one more secondhand orgasm. As far as thinking things through, he concluded the way to get back what he'd once had was simply to begin again. With a new love, a *blind* love. He knew it was not a solution that would make his mother happy. God intended marriage to last for life, she'd probably remind him. For better or worse you promised, she'd say, having explained already that separation was not the will of God and divorce a sin. One of the worst transgressions.

"Tell that to Julia," he'd said then, exasperated. And she did.

His mother reported later: "Such an argument I got from that woman. She tried to convince me there was no God. Can you believe it? It was like listening to one of them ladies on LA Law."

Carlin decided not to wait for the honeymooners. He got dressed and left the rondavel. As he strolled down the pathway to the ocean, the night was bright, clear and sweet smelling. He sat on the pier for hours, watching the waves repeatedly expend themselves on the black beach and deciding, finally, to catch the first plane home and start looking for someone new right away. She would not be a lawyer. An artist might be interesting. A poet, perhaps, or a sculptor. A model would be acceptable, if she wasn't too thin and had much energy. Even the right Avon lady would do.

But not another God-damned stupid lawyer.

HARVEY

"What do you hear from Harvey?" mother asks. Though feeble of body, her mind is a fresh sheet of bond: clean, supple, and sharp enough to cut if not handled properly. There is no need to ask Harvey who.

"I don't hear anything. I don't even know if he's alive, for God's sake."

"Don't use the Lord's name like an infidel," Mother says, dressed to the nines for my Sunday visit to the Golden Sunshine Home. Her velvet dress, its purple nap worn, is without wrinkle. The fake diamond ear rings my father gave her the year before he died, and which she refuses to believe are not genuine, sparkle as her white-haired head bobs. "He's alive," she insists. "I read last week that he's a neurosurgeon at Mount Sinai. Operates on African kings and Hollywood queens."

The message is that Harvey has outdone her son. Again. Or, as she so often said when my report card arrived with its slate of Bs and Cs, "Dennis O'Rourke, you let me down. Don't you know a mother needs to be proud? Your sisters can marry rich men — they're growing up more lovely than I was when I married your father — but what are *you* going to do? I'll bet there's no shame in Harvey's family."

Not likely; Harvey got straight As. Which prompts the question of why he hung around with someone his intellectual inferior. Social inferior, too. My dad was a janitor; his father owned a chain of fancy furniture stores in Toronto. Just about everyone hankered to be Harvey's friend; of what possible worth could I be? I don't know. I only know that Harvey came along while I thrashed about in the waters of adolescence, swirling and black. Perhaps he liked being a lifeguard.

We had nothing more in common than the fact we were fourteen. Harvey was tall and tanned, with bushy eyebrows and black hair that made him look like Eddie Fisher. Young Elizabeth Taylors would clamour for Harvey, not for someone short and freckled-white, with nasty red hair that rebelled against brush and comb.

Harvey caught up with me at the Roxy Theatre on Queen Street as I trudged toward the institution I already hated. "Going to Parkdale Collegiate?" he asked.

"Yeah."

"Me too."

In the air was the leaf-pile odour of autumn. Harvey fell in beside me. "You as nervous as me?"

"Nervous?"

"They say this school's tough. Students drop out. Fifteen percent a year, I heard. For every hundred starting out, only forty-five will graduate."

"Yeah."

I meant yeah I was nervous and yeah many of us would drop out. Whether his calculation was correct was beyond me. Mathematics was not one of my better subjects. Not that I had a good subject. Ma was the one who pushed me on to Parkdale. Personally, I thought high school was a waste of time. High school was for the rich and smart, like Harvey.

Mother spots a wrinkle in her pale purple pantyhose and tugs it out. "Give him a call," she says. She smells like the perfume counter at K Mart.

"What?"

"Call Harvey at the hospital. The boy always liked me, will want to see me, though he'll puke when he sees this dump." Mother points to what she calls the mustard drapes and the ketchup carpet. There is no point reminding her that she chose to leave the apartment my wife and I had built for her. "Listen to your mother," she says. "Call the man."

Harvey, a doctor? His ambition had been to be the new Jack Benny. Of course, my ambition had been to become a famous author, with a Groucho mustache and a Hemingway beard. Maybe no one ever turns into the person he wants to be. "It's been forty years," I say. "Harvey

37

won't remember us."

"Yes he will. Call."

Go figure. The first time I brought Harvey home to work on a science project, Ma looked at him as though he was a bug on her pansies. I hate it when she gets that look; the squinty eyes and stretched-tight lips mean I've done something wrong. After Harvey left, Ma put her hands on her hips and gave one of her precursor sighs, the kind that always makes me think, Oh Shit! That," she groaned, "*that* is your best friend? The one you always talk about?"

"What did you think," I said, "that I'd bring Bing Crosby home?" Ma bought every record this sappy singer made. Plus had his picture on the china cabinet, pipe and all, over which my father draped *The Telegram* or *Liberty Magazine*.

"He's a Jew."

"Who? Bing Crosby?"

The slim line of eyebrow hairs that had escaped Mother's plucking plummeted. "It's not bad enough my son is stupid," she said, her voice gusting with a sound like the time I slashed the principal's tires (because he strapped me for something Annie Kowalski did), "my son is also disrespectful. You watch your mouth, young man. I've washed it with soap before. You're not so big I can't do it again. Now tell me proper, what's the big idea bringing a Jew into our home?"

"Who knows if he's Jewish or not Ma, but if he is, so what?"

Harvey and I went to his house after that, a near-mansion two-storey. I'd never seen such carpets. And living room furniture: dark mahogany tables and striped silk chairs and sofa, all of which his mother kept covered with clear plastic. She reminded us every day we could occupy only his bedroom (where we listened to Peggy Lee and Frank Sinatra) or the basement (where we ping ponged the boredom from our psyches).

"This stuff's from my dad's store," Harvey explained, "and it gets changed twice a year. He'd be furious if anything got damaged." Harvey wasn't much more comfortable in his house than I was, so we found reasons to spend more time at Parkdale. We joined the camera club.

I said, "It'll give us an excuse to take pictures of girls."

Harvey chuckled. "We'll scour the school for models."

"Get them to pose in bathing suits."

"Or nude."

"Have you ever seen a naked woman?" I asked.

"Sure. Haven't you?"

"Where the heck would I get to see a naked woman?"

"Same place as me, in a nudist magazine. I have one at home, stashed under my mattress."

He brought it to school and we locked ourselves in the darkroom to pore over images of naked people, walking and sitting and doing stupid things like playing volleyball. Harvey turned the pages, glancing at me to make sure I didn't wish to linger longer over a particularly healthy body. The second time through the book, a dialogue evolved. What kinds of legs were best? He liked long and thin and pointed to a pair he said were best. I liked them all, but was afraid to say so. Why did some breasts droop while others thrust themselves forward with no sag at all? Why did the men's penises shrivel shamefully between their legs? Harvey speculated: "Maybe you can't get an erection when other men are around. You know, like in the locker room at school."

"A what?"

"An erection. A hard-on."

"Oh, sure," I said, embarrassed by my ignorance.

Never again did we look together at, or talk about, bare body parts, though when we were fifteen we did have a discussion about marriage. Harvey planned to remain a virgin, he said. I nodded. It was an easy decision to make; I expected to go to my grave without a partner, and said so.

"You won't have any trouble getting a woman," Harvey assured me.

"Heck, man, I look like a toad."

"That's the whole point, Denny. Girls *love* toads."

The Mount Sinai Hospital switchboard operator can't put me through because Harvey is in surgery. A robot woman takes a message. Doubt surges: he won't call back because he doesn't remember me; he won't call back because he *does* remember me, a whiny, wild-haired, confidence-lacking youth who tried his patience back then every day of the week. A famous neurosurgeon won't wish to be reminded, especially not by a corporate accountant, not even one who's become Vice President, Finance, of the time he stole a cigar from his father's study.

"Ever smoked a stogie?" Harvey had asked. We were in the darkroom, a space that had once been a cloakroom but now had a red safelight hanging by a black cord and a chipped porcelain sink that backed into one corner with drooling faucets. We peered down that day into a developing tray to see if the pictures we'd taken at a track and field meet were going to turn out. A long-legged girl materialized at the bottom of the pan, her chest straining to reach the finish line ribbon. It was one of Harvey's better photos and made the front page of the school newspaper.

"A stogie?" I said. "Well, not lately."

"I got one for us to try on the way home."

The smoke and the smell of it, when Harvey sucked furiously at one end to get a glow going at the other, remains in my memory.

"This is rotten," he said, handing the cigar over. His scrunched-up face looked as though he'd eaten dog dirt.

"It's okay," I said, puffing like Winston Churchill and wishing the thing didn't feel slimy between my fingers. Though I tried not to inhale, the terrible taste coated my throat and lasted long past supper.

Show business beckoned when we were sixteen. Harvey had always wanted to sing in a barbershop quartet, so we advertised on the school bulletin board for another couple of singers. A few guys, younger than us and tone-deaf, showed up in an unused corner of the cafeteria to sing one verse each of *Sweet Adeline*. Harvey told them we had more people to audition. "Don't call us," he said, smirking across the table, "we'll call you." When they left, he chuckled. "I've always wanted to say that."

"Yeah."

"So, I guess I don't get to sing in a quartet."

"Anybody can have a *regular* quartet," I said. "What you and I have is the only barbershop quartet in the world with just two guys." He giggled the way my youngest sister always did and slapped me hard on the back. Later, we got straw hats and striped shirts and learned *Down By The Old Mill Stream*. We won first place in the talent show comedy category. We hadn't registered as a comedy act, but our feelings weren't hurt and we began to think of ourselves as Abbott and Costello or Laurel and Hardy.

Summer weekends found us scanning the boardwalk at Sunnyside. We looked girls over and talked about them in a private code. "My father says I can have the car tonight," Harvey would say, meaning the girl had an outstanding figure. If I replied, "I'll pay for the gas," it meant I wouldn't kick her out of my bunk, either. You can figure out what it meant when one of us said the car had two flat tires. We went to the Sunnyside pool once but neither of us liked our spindly bodies. Bright-coloured shirts and bell-bottom slacks were better than bathing suits. Harvey taught me how to walk the boardwalk: shoulders shoved back, hands in my pockets, feet sliding forward in a fashionable swagger. He never put me down. Sometimes I even felt his equal.

I won first prize for poetry in the yearbook competition, for writing a clunky allegory about our Prime Minister, Mackenzie King, and for including stuff like *comme il faut*. When I learned I had to read the poem out loud at Assembly, I was horrified. "Everyone will think I'm the biggest jerk in the school," I moaned.

"Not necessarily," Harvey said. He had a plan.

Assembly morning we crept backstage with a Fels Naptha carton containing the outfit he'd put together. Behind a Pirates of Penzance backdrop, he dressed me in red hockey stockings, blue boxer shorts splattered with cherry-red hearts, my dad's work boots and one of his mother's white blouses. He jammed a yellow toque on my head and painted circles on my cheeks with his mother's Max Factor rouge. The Parkdale fire hall had been conned into loaning us an old, hand-cranked siren, and when the principal asked me to come forward, Harvey wound it up as I pranced to the microphone, unrolled the toilet paper on which I'd printed my poem and read with what I thought was an authentic Russian accent. Harvey had rehearsed me for two weeks and it was only later we learned my practiced intonation was more Yiddish than Russian.

The Assembly erupted. Mount Vesuvius. Laughter followed the flowing applause that buried teachers attempting to restore order. For three minutes I was the Volcano God. Then I was hauled into the principal's office for a lecture, a month's worth of detentions and a note to take home. Harvey confessed to being the mastermind of the operation and earned equal punishment, an action that greatly increased my appreciation of his friendship.

Every time the phone in my corner office rings, I think it's Harvey. I pick the receiver up with apprehension; the sound of another voice never fails to prompt disappointment.

Did his mother wonder why he spent so much time with a strange Gentile boy? How did he manage to get *my* mom to see him as a saint? By the time we graduated, Ma would gladly have traded me for Harvey. If he didn't come to the house two or three times a week, she'd demand to know if we'd had a fight. She prophesied, constantly, that he would someday be somebody. "It's not *what* you know in this world," she'd say, "as much as it is *who* you know. Listen to your mother."

Finally, the call arrives. My stomach churns. "Mr. O'Rourke?" asks the voice, deep and resonant, exactly like the old days. "I have a message that you called."

Mr. O'Rourke? Harvey doesn't remember me, that's for certain. The relationship I had thought so strong — he was the brother I'd longed for — had been only a one-sided affair, like the time I fell for Annie Kowalski, a beauty in pleated skirt and saddle shoes, and when I blurted out that I loved her she told me to go steal a dog. Or the time Harvey asked the thin-legged Betty Goodman to go out and she said, "What? Do I look *that* hard up? Give me a break."

The difference, of course, was that Harvey added, "Give you a break? That's what I'm trying to do, Good Looking. You don't see me hitting on any other gorgeous woman around here, do you?" And Betty said, "Okay."

Mr. O'Rourke? He's forgotten our paper route, the largest *Star* route in the city, and how we each did one side of the street, running from house to house, and how we printed flyers on his dad's Gestetner to get new customers. We made enough money for a used Harley-Davidson but neither his parents nor mine would allow us to buy a motorcycle. "Not while the war is on," Mother said, making me truly hate Hitler. Harvey's father pointed out that Artie Shaw never had a bike when he was in school, and when Harvey said, "What's that got to do with the price of cheese in China?" he got grounded.

We gave the money to the Scott Mission. Out of spite. And won Parkdale's Benevolent Medal because of it. Go figure. "We can't accept it," I said.

"False pretenses," Harvey agreed. "That's just not our style." But they gave us the medal anyway, even after we explained we'd only wanted to infuriate our folks.

Mr. O'Rourke? Doesn't Harvey remember he was the one who taught me to look truth straight in the eye? To accept the fact I was short? To understand that it was laziness that caused my low marks? Has he forgotten how he badgered me to abandon my self-pity? How *can* Harvey have forgotten: me, the things we did, the way we felt about each other? The way *I* felt, anyway.

For once, Mother is wrong and I am right. She'll be disappointed, angry, or both, like the time I started to grow a beard but had to shave it off. Her need to have things her own way hasn't diminished with time.

"I don't suppose you remember me," I say into the mouthpiece, hoping he can't hear the heart thumps. "Dennis O'Rourke. We went to school together. A long time ago. Parkdale Collegiate."

"Dennis? The Parkdale Poet? Kowalski's Kid? Of course I remember. How the hell are you, Denny?"

We exchange memories for maybe five minutes before I hear a loudspeaker blaring his name and know Harvey has to go. Before he hangs up, he says we should get together sometime, he really wants to see me again, and I tell him sure, I'll give him a call, maybe next week.

I let go of the telephone, wondering about the report I must now convey to the Golden Sunshine Home. Will I inform Mother that Harvey did not ask about her? Or should I lie, telling her Harvey-the-Neurosurgeon remembers her as his second mother, not afraid, like his first mother, to roll out a piecrust or hang a fly coil in the pantry, or scratch when, and where, she was itchy? Should I tell Mother that Harvey remembers her with fondness but is too busy to visit?

My fingers stroke the side of my face, feel the stubble lurking beneath the skin. It's not a hard decision to make at all. I'll tell her Harvey has forgotten.

COMFORT ZONE

Wesley stopped for gas. It was important to arrive with the tank full, and according to the map Walter had meticulously drawn and mailed last month, the farm was only three miles away.

"Nice trailer," the woman said as she wiped the perspiration from her pink forehead and unscrewed his gas cap.

"Thanks."

It was all he had left, along with the Chevrolet he used as a tow vehicle. They'd sold the house in London and split the proceeds after the break up. Not that there was much cash left for either of them. Irene insisted she be awarded the boat — a thirty-two foot Chris Craft — so he'd agreed to take the trailer. He supposed Irene had gotten the best of the deal — three to one, if he reckoned right — but it was okay; she deserved it, and he'd never liked the water much anyway. Lake Huron, like the ten year span of their marriage, was simply too choppy. Sometimes it got stormier than the Atlantic.

"Can I leave her at the pump while I pick up a few groceries?" Wesley asked the woman. He didn't like being bombarded by the prairie sun. "Or shall I wait until you're done?"

"Leave it," the woman said. "Say, how long is this rig anyway?"

"Thirty-two feet."

It was actually twenty-nine.

No one else was in the hot store. It smelled of old wood and black pepper. He pushed a rusting cart down a narrow aisle, pausing to toss cans of soup and salmon into the basket. Walter was not to feel the brother he hadn't talked to for twenty years would in any way be a burden. Not like the old days, the kid brother hanging around making a pest of himself. This would be different. After he'd written to Walter about the separation, an invitation had arrived for him to visit the farm for a holiday. In accepting, Wesley had spelled out the terms: he would park the trailer for one week in some out-of-the-way spot on the farm and be entirely self-sufficient. He'd written: "The Airstream has a stove, a fridge, water, a bedroom and its own bathroom, so I don't expect to inconvenience your family in any way." This visit would cost his brother nothing; nothing in cash, nothing in aggravation. Still, Wesley wasn't sure now he should have come.

Walter was four years his senior. Of course, he'd been their parents' favourite son. Hadn't he received the best marks in school, collected accolades as an athlete, and never once got into trouble? Walter had been excellent at everything good. The only thing Wesley had been better than average at was being worse than average at everything. He'd never been able to even find his elder brother's shoes, much less fill them, and if one isn't worthy of love then it shouldn't be a surprise if one is not loved.

The woman came inside and waited for him at the cash register. She was fiftyish and plump. As he began unloading the cart onto a plywood counter, she offered a cordial smile.

"See you're from Ontario."

"Yes."

"You staying in Saskatchewan for awhile?"

"Just passing through."

Walter might not want people to know his black sheep brother was in the area. Not that Wesley was a criminal. He just hadn't been able to achieve Walter's own level of accomplishment. His brother was securely married and had three children; Wesley was divorced. Fortunately, he and Irene had chosen not to have a family. Walter owned a huge farm; Wesley wasn't clever enough to mastermind an enterprise of his own. All he could claim now was a five-year-old trailer, a few clothes and some odds and ends.

He'd even failed at something as simple as religion. When, as a child, his brother heeded a Pentecostal evangelist's call, Wesley had stepped forward in the church too. The counsellor dealt with the two of them together so Wesley said the same things Walter said and shook his head in harmony. The soul-saving experience had stuck with Walter through

Sunday School and on into full adult membership in the congregation, but Wesley's salvation had dribbled away. For years his parents nagged at him "to put things right with God," but he never returned to the church. There was no evidence God loved him any more than anyone else did. No matter how hard he tried, Wesley could not please, could not consistently be good, the way Walter was.

The woman smiled again. "See you're a bachelor."

"Pardon?"

"Tell from the stuff. Men's meals. Quick and easy."

"I travel alone," he said, hoping his voice didn't betray his feelings.

The concession was clearly marked. The road, though narrow and covered with fresh gravel, was flat, and burrowed in no-nonsense fashion straight through the wheat fields. Ontario roads had a habit of meandering up and down, and curving around. As long as he drove slowly on these prairie stones, he'd have no difficulty handling the Airstream.

The map was Scotch-taped to the dash and in his mind he checked off the landmarks as he passed them: train tracks, an abandoned church, a charred barn. He was grateful there was no other traffic to spray him with gravel or cover the car and trailer with stone dust. The least he could do was arrive clean.

Walter's driveway swung around a half-filled slough, green at the shoreline, then edged past a stand of scrawny trees. Wesley stopped midway between a frame house and a row of galvanized-metal granaries. He stepped out of the car. A GMC pickup, red, nosed toward the back door. On top of a child's wagon, a grey cat slept, its tail hanging over the edge, twitching in the midday heat. Wesley wondered if the house was a hired man's home. The paint was so badly faded it was impossible to tell what colour the siding had once been.

"Hello. You must be Wesley."

He spun around and saw a woman rising from the garden. Tall. Shorts and a sleeveless cotton blouse over slender limbs, freckled white. Her hair, cut short, was the colour of the dirt smudge on her cheek.

He said, "Yes, I am. Wesley, I mean."

"I'm so glad to finally meet you. I'm Alice." She took a quick step and put her thin arms around him. "Walter's out checking on a new calf but he should be back soon. He's eager to see you. Hasn't talked about anything else for weeks."

The hug was a shock. Though apparently natural for her, quick and spontaneous, the embrace both surprised and embarrassed him. She'd been working hard in the searing sun and her smell was strong. He disengaged himself.

"Where do you want me to park the trailer?"

"How about over there, beneath the trees? Walter has electricity there for you. I've got a fresh jug of lemonade in the refrigerator when you get settled."

The yard was large enough for Wesley to circle around. He breathed easier. He wasn't good at backing the trailer, particularly with someone else watching. The curved aluminum shell had a will of its own, especially when being forced into a tight spot, and appeared no more willing to yield control to Wesley than anything else. Why was it that when he wanted the Airstream to go right, it usually backed left? Sometimes it didn't seem to matter which way he twisted the steering wheel. The trailer did exactly what it wanted to do. Frustrated, he called the damn thing Irene.

Walter wouldn't have had such trouble. He'd always been totally in control. Basketballs and hockey pucks went where Walter directed. Teachers and parents agreed with his assumptions, as though under a spell. Friends were quick to follow Walter's proposals. For Wesley, however, then as now, events happened willy nilly, without pattern or order, unresponsive to his efforts. He'd never been able to control anything. Whatever happened, good or bad, was inevitable. Que Sera Sera, as Doris Day once sang on their big Philco radio.

Parked at last, he was inside the trailer, opening the windows, when Walter's voice boomed through the screen door. His baritone hadn't changed a bit.

"You inside this contraption, Wes?"

"Come on in, Wally."

The Airstream shivered as Walter opened the door and stepped

48

inside. Wesley had forgotten to put stabilizer jacks under the four corners. Stupid. He'd so wanted to make a good impression.

Walter was not as tall as he remembered, and he was bald. His eyebrows had grown bushy and grey. The skin of his face, sun-darkened and wrinkled, had turned into leather. How many identities are one allowed in a lifetime?

"It's good to see you again."

Walter held out a hand the size of a catcher's mitt. "You haven't changed a bit, Wes. Still look like a movie star. So, how the heck are you?"

Wesley took the hand. The power he remembered was still there. "Fine. Thanks for letting me come. This is great."

"Wanna see a new calf? Just arrived. If we hurry we can get there before the mother finishes eating the after-birth."

Wesley shook his head. "I don't think so. You know how queasy I am, fainting at the first sign of blood."

Walter, like their mother, had a clinical fascination with bones, bruises and blood, and everyone had expected him to become a doctor. Wesley wondered if his mother was disappointed. She'd counted on her favourite son becoming a famous surgeon. She'd never said anything about becoming a farmer.

Walter said, "Well, come on in the house, then. We can have some lemonade and look at pictures while Alice gets supper ready. I got a bunch of photographs down from the attic."

What Wesley really wanted was a cold beer but that was against Walter's religion. "Can we do that later? I'm sorry, Wally, but I'm really stressed out from the long drive. My head feels like a cabbage, so if you don't mind I'll maybe just go for a bit of a walk, stretch my legs, see if the fresh air will clear out my brain."

"Sure. I promised Alice I'd clean out the barn, anyway. 'Sposed to have it done before you got here, actually, so you go ahead and relax. We got a whole week to visit." He threw his arms around Wesley, gave him a powerful squeeze, and was gone, leaving behind only his tangy farm smell: feed, cattle, salt blocks, earth. What had his brother smelled on him? Printer paper? Cathode rays?

He picked up his camera and hiked toward a back field, deciding without fully understanding why that he needed to capture images that would remind him of this visit. Though the photographs would only be of split-rail fences and John Deere farm equipment, they'd prompt him to remember he had family, people who knew he was alive, who wanted to spend time with him. He'd show the photographs of his brother's farm to his coworkers so they, too, would understand he was connected to something more important than a keyboard. His pictures would be proof that Irene had been unable to sever his ties.

Wesley walked with the black Nikon banging against his chest for ten minutes. The field was a pasture, though not, he suspected, a very good one. Weeds choked the grass. Stones littered the ground: most on the surface, some partly buried, others just beneath the surface; the hardness of the earth beneath Wesley's feet assured him they were there. Cakes of cattle dung baked in the sun. Flies followed, buzzing about his face the way thoughts banged inside his head. Why defer Walter's offer to examine old photos? Why was Walter's house — and wife — so plain? Why had Walter's hug made him uncomfortable? There might have been good reason to feel strange about the embrace of a woman he'd never met before, but surely there was no reason to wince at physical contact with his own flesh and blood.

Had Walter hugged him before? Not that he could remember. Walter had detested him, so why would he? Nor could Wesley recall being held by his mother and father, though he was certain they must have done so, sometime. It's what parents do; an accepted responsibility. Relationships impose certain obligations, though Irene had assured him that true intimacy was intellectual, not physical. She'd said, "It's what sets man apart from the animals."

Wesley stopped as a blue jay perched on a fence post. The brilliance of its colour prompted him to raise the Nikon to his eye. He saw nothing. Cursing his stupidity, he removed the lens cap. The bird was too small in the viewfinder; it wouldn't show up well in prints passed to coworkers. He moved slowly toward the jay, not wanting to startle it. There were five posts between them and everything was all right. Then four. Just as he crept up to the third post, the blue jay took flight.

Immediately five posts separated them again.

Wesley moved slower this time. He kept the camera to his eye. Four posts. Half way to the third. He stopped to let the bird get used to him. A minute later he took another step. Then a half step. It was going well now. He could see the image of the blue jay growing larger in the viewfinder, though still not large enough to impress anyone back in London. Another tiny step, then another. Just as he reached the third post, the bird fluttered away again. After a half hour, Wesley called the blue jay Irene and gave up. The third post was the perimeter of the bird's comfort zone. He was unable to get past it.

How was he supposed to act? He had no idea. What does one do to become acceptable? Because acceptance was surely the precursor to love. He'd never been able to determine exactly what behaviour made that miracle happen. Everything he could think of he'd tried: patience, tenderness, attentiveness, acquiescence, acceptance. And trust. He'd done more than his share of the housework and had worked hard at being non-sexist. He'd never refused to let Irene buy anything she wanted. He'd even given his brown suit to the Salvation Army after she told him that brown was bland. All his earth-tone ties had gone, too, but nothing had changed.

Why couldn't the damned blue jay just sit still and understand he did not wish to hurt it?

What photographs would he have to look at with Walter? Not, he hoped, the one taken by an uncle. They were eight and four, back then, Walter tall and good looking and confident, while Wesley was stunted, clothed in baggy hand-me-downs. In the picture, his ears were immense, his nose Pinocchio-long, and their uncle had said, "Geez, Sarah-Jane, I'd keep this child of yours out of the damned barn, that's for sure. The cows get a look at this kid, they'll stop giving milk. I've never seen anyone so damned ugly in my whole life."

Wesley started back, even though he didn't wish to revisit childhood. Accepting his brother's invitation to visit the farm had been another mistake. The trailer hadn't been unhitched; perhaps he could climb back into the Chevrolet and drive his world away. Walter might be relieved, might only have brought him west because of some misguided sense of obligation. Wesley would do both of them a favour.

When he arrived at the Airstream, the top of his head baked and the underarms of his shirt sweat-wet, his nose tingling from the smell of fresh-cut hay, a boy was fingering the rivets that fastened the aluminum panels together. He yanked his hand away when he saw Wesley.

"I wasn't doing nothing, Uncle Wes. Honest. I was just looking."

The boy was nine or ten and looked exactly the way Wesley remembered his brother, except for his eyes. They were softer, lighter, more gentle; they were the eyes of Alice. Wesley nodded, as if to say it was all right. He stepped into the trailer and the boy followed.

"This is rad. You really *are* rich. You got a chesterfield and curtains in here, and everything. And a Sony TV. Wow! Is it colour?"

"Yes."

"It figures. We only got an old black and white. Is it true what my dad says, that you're a computer expert?"

"There are lots of people smarter than I, but I do work in data processing."

"My dad says you can make a computer do exactly what you want it to do."

"Well, it's easy to make a machine behave. A lot easier than people, anyway." Wesley smiled. "You haven't told me yet what your name is."

"You haven't asked me yet."

"Okay, what's your name?"

"Wesley." The boy grinned. He was a charmer, just the way Walter had been.

"Wesley?"

"Yep. Named after you, my ma says."

Wesley put on a clean shirt. "Can I take a picture of you?" he asked the boy. A photograph of his namesake would be better to show than a neurotic blue jay. He reached for the camera but the boy shook his head.

"Nope."

"You don't want me to take your picture?"

"Nope."

"Why not?"

"You got a timer on that thing?"

"Yes."

"You got a tripod?"

"I do."

The boy grinned again. "Set it up so you can take a picture of both of us. Together. Outside the trailer."

He set the camera on the tripod, pushed the button and scurried back to stand beside his nephew. The camera clicked. The boy said, "Can we do another one, Uncle Wes? For me? To show the kids at school?"

"Sure," Wesley said, "and then maybe you could go get your mom and dad so we can take a picture of all of us. The whole family." He wondered whether he could put his arm around the boy. Not just yet, certainly. Perhaps he would be able to do it before he left.

If not tomorrow, then the day after that.

NOTHING PERSONAL

This morning I stood in front of the full-length mirror in my bedroom. Naked. I looked at myself head on, frowned, then turned sideways. My profile was no better, not even when I sucked in my stomach and jammed my shoulders back. I clenched and raised one fist, squinting to find nothing more than a feeble bicep. I don't know why I did this; for a lifetime I've avoided mirrors. You would too if you had red hair, pasty white skin splattered with freckles and a ski-slope nose. Of course, my hair isn't really red any more, except in that one cluster of pubic curls no one else will ever see. What's left of the public mane is now a washed-out silver; my mother, if she were still alive, would call it tattle-tale-grey, a disappointing colour. Perhaps that's why I shivered in front of the mirror this morning: not because I've grown white and wrinkled and sprouted a shameful pot belly, but because today — my birthday — I arrived at the fulcrum of my life, the turning point from which all I can see is the time left. From here on it's downhill.

For most of my life I yearned to be older. When I was six I refused to wear short pants, quite certain corduroy trousers made me look more grown up. I never understood why the boys in my Sunday School class whined about having to wear a tie one day a week. Dressing up in a white cotton shirt and one of my father's hand-painted ties made me feel like an adult. Content. On family visits to my uncle's farm, I shunned the uncivilized cousins who congregated in the yard, preferring to park in the sitting room with my aunt's collection of picture plates from around the world, mounted high on all four walls. The parlour was the place where the chattering adults settled.

I loved it when my aunt purred, "My, isn't Charles the perfect little gentleman."

I hated it when father hollered, "Go outside and play with the rest of the damn kids!"

I wept once, realizing that I was in the way, had been a disappointment to my father one more time, that the topic of conversation had
veered adultward and I was merely one of the insignificant offspring.
Mother took me aside to explain it was only that father wanted me to
have lots of fresh air and exercise, but I knew better. I'd heard my uncle
say it; I was redundant. I didn't know what that meant, but I was sure
it wasn't anything to be proud of.

In high school I eschewed the juvenile activities: certain jock sports,
cruising for girls, creating graffiti, stealing chocolate bars, letting air
out of tires and talking back to teachers. Instead, I joined the debating
team, became a member of the chess club and was asked to manage
the yearbook staff. No one else wanted to do it. That was all right with
me. I felt older, more responsible, near-adult. I wore a tie every day.
I pretended not to know — or care — that others said I was a stuck-up
jerk, in love with myself, and I couldn't explain to anyone, myself
included, that the reason I avoided the most popular endeavour was
fear of failure. I wasn't good enough to do the things done so well by
those I longed to call my friends. I couldn't hit a baseball, catch a
football, or make myself attractive to girls, and I didn't care to steal,
vandalize, or sass elders, my teachers included.

That urgent drive to grow up kept me from college. My mother let
me know she was baffled (her word, not mine) by my decision, but I
simply hankered to get into the work place sooner: to earn money,
live in a place of my own, wear wire-rim glasses, smoke a pipe, go to
movies of my own choice and have an old Ford, all of which I did by
the time I was nineteen, plus grow a mustache. I shaved that off,
though, when it turned out to be nothing more than a patch of ugly
red bristles. I stopped smoking, too, unable to enjoy the taste of
tobacco. For a while I carried my hand-carved Indian-head pipe
around, using it to point with or to otherwise keep my large and
awkward hands occupied, but finally I gave that up, too. A brown felt
fedora, the kind my father always wore, became part of my wardrobe
for a year or so, but when the wind wafted it away one spring I didn't
replace it.

There was another reason for avoiding college. I'd never been able to live up to my father's expectations for academic excellence. He demanded a lot (for my own good, he told me regularly), but I grew weary of never being good enough. When I brought home a seventy average, pleased for not falling behind the rest of my class, he insisted I achieve seventy-five. Instead of congratulating me when my struggling finally produced a seventy-six average, he waggled his black-topped head (I don't know where my red hair came from because mother was a brunette) and complained that I hadn't put forth enough effort to earn an eighty. As an incentive to excel, father promised ten dollars for a mark of eighty, one hundred dollars for a ninety, and one thousand dollars for bringing home a perfect-in-every-subject report card. He never had to pay a dime.

I stopped going to church after I left home. That surely disappointed the Lord as much as my other Christian failures: the occasional outburst of gluttony, my somewhat regular willingness to take the name of Christ in vain, my constant lustful thoughts about the pleasant clerk in our office, Ellie Smith. However, the situation was, to use my mother's favourite expression, tit for tat; God had disappointed me, too. It was cruel of Him to create such horrid hair, thin legs, squeaky voice and long nose; the list goes on, but you get the idea. If God had not let *me* down, I would have felt worse than I did about being a disappointment to Him.

Anyway, after half a century of wanting to look older, here I am yearning to be young again. There's nothing about the aging process that will make anyone want or need me now. Decay destroys romance, doesn't it? No one loves the elderly. Does that sound as if I'm feeling sorry for myself, full of self pity? Let me point out that for the past year I've gone to a fitness club, one of those places filled with the latest chromed-metal and black-leather body bashing machines. Father always said God helps those who help themselves and I've truly done all that could be done to fight off the onslaught of time: changed my diet, climbed the stairs to my office instead of taking the elevator, cut down on the drinking, and so on. Unfortunately, none of it was enough to prevent Ellie, my good wife of twenty years, from leaving me last month. Without warning, I might add.

Not that I blame her. Ellie was, and is, a remarkably fine woman. She's an excellent mother to our two girls. While I was out working to pay off the mortgage and keep food on the table, she cooked and cleaned, helped with the school work and did all those other things perfect wives manage to do. She never once said no when I had a physical need. Although I was grateful for her accommodation, I felt badly that my own performance was never good enough to inspire passion. Ellie must have been disappointed. I can't think of any other reason for her to leave.

Back when money was tighter than it is now, she saved cents-off coupons and hunted for food specials. She sent me to certain gas stations to collect free glasses or garbage bags or screwdrivers, and whenever my company sent me across the continent to solve a branch plant accounting problem, Ellie made sure I collected frequent-flyer points so we could enjoy a winter holiday in Florida. She never once disappointed me. Not in any way worth recounting.

Ellie's father died of Alzheimer's a few years ago; perhaps she thought my strange behaviour was a sign I had it, too. She wouldn't be able to go through that ordeal again. Of course, it wasn't Alzheimer's.

I don't know why I developed a crush on the young fitness instructor at the exercise club. Becca was attractive enough, I suppose, and had a shape that every woman dreams about. Well, the truth is I have no idea what women dream about; Becca had a figure that every *man* dreams about. She was no dummy, either. A university graduate, she could discuss, with intelligence, everything from world affairs to domestic violence. It was Becca's wonderful caring that got to me, though, rather than her IQ. She was determined to keep me going, to offset my discouragement at not achieving goal-weight right away, to inspire me to continue pumping, cycling, stretching and rowing. There were many good looking body builders in that gym (you could find one in front of any club mirror, it seemed); Becca chose to spend more of her time helping me, and I loved her for it. Never once did she indicate I'd fallen short of her expectations. Becca touched me a lot: on the arm, on the shoulder, on the thigh once, always with great tenderness. My skin tingled where her fingers touched; she raised the hairs on the back of my neck.

"You're good for me," I told her once, sweat dripping from my brow.

Becca beamed. "I'm glad, Charles." No perspiration was evident above or below the black velvet band that kept her buttercup hair from falling in front of morning glory blue eyes. The scent of Becca was that of baby talcum, clean and comforting in the club's great hall of deliberate sweat.

Breathing hard, I said, "I'd have given up a long time ago if it hadn't been for you."

"They told me you renewed your membership for another year. I'm proud of you."

Becca became my fountain of youth. I could think of nothing else but going to the club. My step was lighter. Even if I didn't look different, I felt younger. The harder I worked, the more my muscles ached but the less it mattered. I bought a new workout suit, the kind more youthful members wore: neon bright, skin tight and expensive. The time wasn't right to tell Becca about a marriage gone stale, that great aging accelerator, but I began searching for the proper words and filed them carefully away for future use. I knew she'd understand. I'd never been promiscuous, had never made a pass at my secretary, even though she's a lovely person, nor had I entertained any thought of fooling around with one of the female staff members of Alternative Housing Inc., the non-profit group that had asked me to sit on its board a few years ago. Some people volunteer for a night out, to get away from boring or abusive parents or partners, to have a fling; that wasn't the case with me. I just wanted to help someone: single parents, the handicapped, the chronically unemployed. So you see, Becca was the only woman I ever fell in love with, after Ellie.

I got a bad case of tennis elbow — bursitis — and had to wear an elastic bandage while exercising. Bless her, Becca never mentioned my badge. Attacks of insomnia came with increasing regularity. I lay awake nights, wanting Becca but not having the courage to tell her. Nor did I wish to hurt the woman who'd accepted me so long ago, the one person who understood back then how I found it easier to get along with numbers than I did with people. Numbers are predictable. They don't require me to compete for their attention. Numbers adhere to an easy-to-understand logic. As long as I follow the rules, I can neither disappoint nor be disappointed.

When Becca finally occupied so much of my heart that I knew I couldn't live without her, I began to wonder if written words might also be like numbers, accurate and understandable, performing as their creator intended, producing an answer that could be relied upon. After much thought, I decided to write a letter. Afraid it might fall into the wrong hands and embarrass Becca, and me, I manufactured the letter by looking into a mirror instead of at the paper. It took practice. For the first few days, my brain ignored the reflected image, causing my clumsy hand to swoop right instead of left, but gradually I became adept at reverse writing. Since I wouldn't be able to reveal the reading code in the letter itself, I prepared Becca in advance.

"Should you find something in your life incomprehensible," I told her, "try looking at it in a mirror." I was pedalling at the time. Hard. The pain in my chest was so bad I wondered if I was having a heart attack. I imagined Becca looking down at me in the coffin, tears dribbling down her baby-soft cheeks.

She put her slender fingers on my shoulder, smiled prettily, and said, "You should be able to pedal for at least another five minutes, Charles. Your stamina has improved nicely. Really. I'm proud of you."

It was another week before my reverse handwriting was good enough. I sealed my message in an envelope, wrote Becca's name, frontwards this time, and left it for her at the desk. Instead of exercising in the club, I went for a walk, thinking about my backward words. I pictured Becca standing before the mirror in her bedroom, nude perhaps, holding my letter up to the mirror. Would she think me clever for encoding the message? *.uoy evol I* She surely wouldn't be surprised to learn how I felt about her; that must have been evident months ago. I hadn't mentioned our age difference. Would it matter? Nor had I offered to divorce Ellie, a notion that Becca would surely see as premature. She was, after all, a sensitive woman. I closed the note by proposing we have dinner together to discuss the situation, to chart our future. I wondered what she'd wear. I'd never seen Becca in high heels and a dress. Would she wear make-up and jewelry? I hoped not; I loved her unspoiled.

Ellie was waiting on the sofa when I got home.

"Who is Becca Crawlinski?" she asked. Her arms and legs were crossed.

"My aerobics instructor at the club."

"I see. Well, Ms Crawlinski called to say she can't make it for dinner. Maybe next week, she said."

I felt a wobble in my knees. My face flushed, my heart thumped. As though I'd just completed a half hour on the rowing machine, I could barely breathe. Words on paper hadn't behaved like numbers. Before I could think of a sane reply, the doorbell rang. It was a taxi driver, come to take my wife away. I'd missed the suitcases in the hall. Ellie said, "I don't need this shit."

Though we've talked on the telephone since then, mostly about alimony, that was the last time I saw her. The girls, whom I expected would engineer a reconciliation, did not, though they call every week. They've told me, several times, how disappointed they are. I let them down, as well as their mother, they explained. Of course, they're right.

I guess I was pretty much of a disappointment for Becca, too. Ask yourself: what kind of woman would tell a man's wife she'd agreed to go out with her husband? A smart woman who understands the best way to shut down an emerging Romeo is to make public his ignoble secret. It worked. And since it was obvious Becca didn't care for me, saw me only as a dues-paying customer, I stopped going to the fitness club.

I didn't quit eating greens or climbing stairs, though. I hated living with an aging man and figured no one else would enjoy sitting around waiting for the funeral, either. I might not make myself much better, but I had to prevent myself from getting much worse. Which is to say, visibly older. I knuckled down at the office, working harder than ever. Since there was nothing — and no one — to go home for, I remained at the plant, often until midnight. A lot of work got done. Certain the firm appreciated my dedication, I waited, more or less patiently, for my next promotion and salary increase. I waited right up to the day the company laid me off.

"I'm sorry, Charles," my boss said, "but there's nothing personal in this. The corporation is restructuring and down-sizing, trimming the fat, learning to operate more efficiently. It's essential to our survival." Fat? My sixteen-hour work days were fat?

I thought of the model airplane I'd constructed when I was ten: hundreds of intricate balsa wood struts, painstakingly cut with a razor blade, meticulously glued together according to a hazy template and sparse instructions, then the fuselage covered carefully with tissue paper. The propeller was wound counter clockwise, with the exact number of elastic-band revolutions called for, and then, with great excitement, my airplane was thrust into the sky. My pride soared, high and graceful. The satisfaction was immense, intense. Suddenly, the airplane lost power and dived, crashing nose first, smashed beyond repair. Dead.

"You must have done something wrong," my father said when I laid the corpse on our dining room table. "It shouldn't have done that. Not the first time out. It isn't even windy out there." I never built another plane.

Not one of the fifty companies I sent a resume to required an old accountant. Only three acknowledged my applications. I spent more time at the decrepit house that served as headquarters for Alternative Housing Inc. Because one of the resource people was away on maternity leave, I was allowed to help, interviewing shelter applicants, calling the Salvation Army or The Mission, arguing on the telephone with a burnt-out clerk at city hall. I worked in what had once been a dining room. A tarnished brass chandelier dangled above my desk. The flowered wallpaper was older than I: faded, dirty and torn. The floorboards were wide and worn. An ancient mirror, splotched where the silver backing had fallen off, was framed by an ornate, once-gold frame. I was careful not to look at the mirror unless the angle was large enough to insure the reflected image didn't include me. Facing myself was beyond my capability.

The house had a musty odour; the smell of advanced age. The roof leaked. Several panes of glass were cracked. The foundation had settled more on one side than the other so that if you dropped your pencil on the floor it rolled away from you. Still, the old house served its purpose well enough and no one complained, myself included. I was grateful for something useful to do. One afternoon, between clients, the executive director dropped in to see me.

She said, "I feel guilty, Charles."

"Guilty?"

"We're taking up so much of your time it must be impossible for you to look for work."

"The city is splattered with my resumes," I said. "And I check the want ads every night, so there's nothing to feel guilty about."

"You've eased our load. You fit in well here, and our clients love your patience, your understanding, your maturity. They say you don't treat them as numbers in a computer. They feel comfortable with you."

I was too embarrassed to look directly at the executive director so I watched her profile in the mirror. It framed her nicely, like a television screen. She was about the age of my oldest daughter. "Thank you," I mumbled.

"Charles, let me get to the point. We can't pay much, and we know you'll have to leave when a good job comes along, but we'd be thrilled to have you on staff, part of our family, for as long as you can stay."

I was flattered, since I'd had no training for the job. All I'd really done was use a bit of common sense. "Let me talk to Ellie," I said. "I'll give you an answer tomorrow." I didn't explain I had support payments to make.

After the director left my office, I sat alone for a few minutes. Had I disappointed Ellie and the girls again? Should I have been more aggressive in my job search? Done more than mail out resumes? If I took the Alternative Housing job, would I let the agency down? Fail to serve a truly needy person?

On the way to get my next client I paused at the antique mirror to make sure my hair was in place and my nose was clean. Mother is the one who taught me the importance of checking your face before showing up in public; you don't want people to see an ink smudge on your cheek or food between your teeth. I also took a moment to practice the smile I try to give each of these troubled folk who comes for help.

Ellie's the one who explained to me how much better a person looks when he doesn't frown.

RETIREMENT DAY

The bedroom window is open. The sun wonders if it is entitled to sleep in on this long-awaited day. Sparrows insist their benefactor shine as scheduled. It does. The alarm clock clangs. Unnecessarily, for John More has been awake for hours, unsettled by yet another dream.

An earthquake, this time. The ground splits in two at his feet, buildings topple, his most precious possessions tumble, one by one, into a frightening chasm. His twelve-band Oceanic Short Wave Receiver. His books: *Cat's Eye*, *The Progress of Love*, *Who Do You Think You Are?* He cries out but no one hears. He runs flat out, heart pumping, lungs wheezing, to the single place in the world where help might be available, only to discover that the bridge to there has been swallowed up, too. The isolating river remains, more savage than ever. Office buildings glisten on the other side, but the earthquake has cut him off.

"Wake up, John."

"I'm awake."

"So get up. You don't wanna be late on your last damn day, do you?"

"No."

"I suppose I could get up and make breakfast, if you really want me to."

"No thanks."

"Whatever. And before I forget, Happy Birthday."

He slithers out of bed into the cool May morning, sets his callused feet on the hardwood floor. Like chickens scratching for food, his toes search for slippers. He yanks his terrycloth robe (yellow, his Christmas gift from Betsy) out of the closet, not caring that its hanger rattles on the metal rod. He jabs his thin arms into the wide openings.

Sixty-five.

How can he have grown so old so quickly? Only yesterday he

graduated with a head bursting with dreams. He'd be president of his own world-class company, highly respected by competitors and much loved by his employees. He'd be wealthy: homes, yachts, expensive cars, a private helicopter. A beautiful woman would abandon her movie career to bear and nurture his children and dispel his frightening sense of isolation, the dark loneliness he'd endured as a child and a teen; he'd been unprepared for all of that to overflow the banks of his youth.

The coffee is ready, switched on by the timer fifteen minutes before the alarm. The rich aroma inundates the kitchen, blends with sunshine driving through the gingham curtains and splattering onto the kitchen table. He pours a glass of orange juice, drops a slice of seven-grain bread into the toaster, retrieves a tub of fat-free margarine from the fridge. He swallows his vitamin capsule.

He should have accepted Betsy's offer to get up. It's too late now. Not that it matters about having to make breakfast. He doesn't mind that but does hate eating alone, shouldn't have been forced to make that decision. A woman who cares would rise without question, would long for his companionship, consider it a privilege to be with him. Betsy never had, never would. Yet from tomorrow on they will be together every hour of every day.

He turns on the shower. Discards his robe. Avoids looking at his thin body in the full-length mirror on the bathroom door. Tests the water temperature. Steps into the driving heat. Soaps. Wishes Betsy had unexpectedly appeared in the shower beside him at least once during the forty-five years of their marriage. He'd crept in with her once, a month after the honeymoon. She locked the bathroom door after that.

He towels himself dry. Pads naked into the bedroom. Selects a white cotton shirt, his blue pin-striped suit, a plain blue tie. Last night, before watching The National, he polished his black shoes. He'll stop at the car wash so his navy Chevrolet will be clean on this final work day. He may only have risen to the rank of division manager, and never could capture the courage to become an entrepreneur, but he can't be faulted for failing to look like a professional manager. He has never had a hair out of place or arrived at the office with a spot on his tie or shineless shoes. Not before he fell in love with Heather O'Toole. Certainly never after.

The marketing manager smiles in the company parking lot. "Good morning, Mr. More."

"Hello Chad. How are you this morning?"

He knows the first name of every employee in the company. He's aware of who is married and who is not, who has children and how many, though he doesn't keep track of ages and names. He knows which men and women have marital problems and has counselled many of them, told them how important communication is to a relationship, but he doesn't advise completely candid conversation. Total disclosure may backfire.

Still, communication is the key, along with accepting your partner as he or she may be. That's important, he tells the youngsters who come for help. Couples are still together today because of the advice of John More. He once received a thank you card on an employee's fifth wedding anniversary. The credit for saving the relationship was his, the young woman had written. He wonders why it's so much easier to give advice than it is to take it.

He hopes the company will present him with a fine gift. One that will impress Betsy and let her know how important he is. The staff may have taken up a collection; it's the custom. That gift may be significant in conveying a message to his wife. She expects the company will give him a watch, but thinks people generally are cold and uncaring, unappreciative of what others do. Betsy thinks John has wasted his time being interested in, and involved with, his staff. She's not a believer in good works. Says people do things for their own benefit, to make themselves feel good.

If the gifts he receives today aren't impressive enough, he'll buy something on the way home. Last night he got out the Jarman shoe box he'd used for years to store one bill of some denomination each pay day, more when he could, unsure what his hoard would accomplish but certain it would be useful one day. Some of the money has King George's picture on it, some Queen Victoria's. He hadn't counted it for a long time; hadn't wanted to be disappointed at how little he'd accumulated over so many years. He'd been surprised last night to discover that the shoe box contained more than fifteen thousand dollars. He'd transferred the cache to his briefcase.

He is certain the president doesn't expect him to put in a full day of work on his retirement day but he's always given a day's work for a day's pay. That's what had moved him as far ahead as he'd come. Lunch hour will be long enough to clean out his desk: mementos of the past, relics from another era. Whatever has value — the gold letter opener, perhaps — he'll give to Heather, recognition for her years of devoted service. She's more than a secretary. Devoted, as well as competent. She doesn't know how he feels. A professional doesn't fall in love with a subordinate. If he does, the emotions must be stifled.

He closes the door to his office. Sits behind his scratched and scruffy desk. Heather told him once it was too small for a man of such importance, that he should request the same glossy walnut suite the company's new MBAS command, complete with credenza and padded side chairs. He'd replied that he thought such furniture ostentatious and hardly suited to the John More management style.

He opens the leather-covered folder that houses his yellow scratch pad with the blue lines. Writes *Heather*. Picks up a red ball-point and draws a heart. Overlaps this with a second heart. Changes to the black pen again. Writes *John*. Perhaps this is the day to tell Heather O'Toole he's loved her all these years, that he appreciates the interest she's shown, her ability to make him feel good when the world conspires to put him down: her birthday cards, the get well messages, the feedback of company rumours, her wise advice on office politics.

It's his final day. What can the consequences be of telling Heather how he feels, that he ached to hold her close a thousand times, dreamed every night about sailing off to a tropical island with her? Betsy hates sailing.

Heather isn't the movie star he desired. Though pleasant, she's plain. Her figure is average. Of course, he's less a prize: thin, wrinkled, nearly bald now. Would she remind him of the quarter century spread in their ages? Or the tall, wavy-haired man who'd wed her a decade ago?

Or is it possible Heather does love him?

No. She only did what she had to do to advance her career; be nice to the boss to keep the salary increases coming. John More is no more important to Heather than he is to anyone else.

She knocks lightly, then glides in with the morning mail.

He says, "Good morning, Heather."

"Good morning, Mr. More. Not so good actually, for us. It's your last day."

He's pleased to see she is wearing the Nova Scotia plaid skirt he likes so well, and the navy blazer. She's not fond of the outfit, he knows, but he once commented that he liked it. Heather remembered.

"You'll get along fine without me."

She shakes her head and the dark curls bounce. "I don't know how we'll get along without you."

She looks better this morning than she ever has. The truth is Heather O'Toole is not plain. Why had he thought she was? She's lovely. Movie star superb.

"I'll miss you, Heather."

"And we'll miss you, Mr. More."

She leaves quietly, way up on her high heels, and closes the door softly behind her. All right, he won't tell her of his love. It was a stupid idea anyway. But today *is* the day to tell Hartlieb he's a jerk. The president has used and abused him for years. Forced him to do the dirty work and get blamed for it. Worse, Hartlieb has always taken the glory for John's best ideas.

Surviving under the president's thumb wasn't a matter of courage, or a lack thereof. One is inhibited in these matters for fear of losing one's livelihood. One behaves as someone else expects him to behave because there's no reasonable alternative. The children had to be supported while they were growing up. And Betsy refused to go back to work even after their last son left home. John More had responsibilities all these years. A real man honours his commitments.

But on his retirement day, why not tell the truth? He hates the man's guts. The staff will cheer. They'll remember their old manager as feisty. Yes, that's what he'll do.

The public address system makes the announcement at four o'clock. "All staff gather in the lunchroom. We wish to pay our respects to Mr. John More, our division manager, on his final day with the company."

He makes one last inspection of the desk. The drawers are empty now and clean. He wiped them with a lemon-oil-soaked cloth he brought in a plastic bag. There was nothing of value to leave for Heather. The letter opener wasn't gold, was littered with advertising, would have been an insult. He'll buy her a book — a Sharon Butala, perhaps — and send it to her with a note. Perhaps he can write what he cannot say. She'll weep to discover he has loved her all along. If only she'd known, she'll think, if only she'd known.

They applaud as he enters. He smiles. Hopes his bearing is regal, yet appropriately humble. The pompous-ass president signals for him to come over. Puts a pudgy arm around his shoulders and coughs. "We are gathered here today to pay tribute to a man who has devoted his life to this company and to the people in it. John More is, without doubt, the best manager this division ever had."

Applause. Too bad Betsy can't hear it.

"He deserves a break after all these years, and time for himself, time to be with his lovely wife, time to go fishing, or shopping, or writing a book, or whatever it is he wants to do, and just so John won't forget us, I want to present to him this gorgeous, gold, quartz, hand-tooled and suitably engraved watch."

More applause. A handshake. John wonders if a speech is expected. If this is the time for him to step forward and put his hate for Hartlieb into words.

He can't do it. He really is a coward. The applause subsides as Heather O'Toole steps forward. There are tears in the corners of her brown eyes. "I want to tell you, Mr. More — John — everyone here has such a high regard for you. As a manager, as a person, as a friend."

Applause. Twice that offered for Hartlieb. And more tears.

"It was difficult trying to decide what to get to show how much we think of you."

He doesn't hear the words that follow, doesn't see clearly through his tears the television set that somebody wheels into the room. Heather hugs him. Her body is warm and firm. Her black hair smells like a meadow at midnight. He can't remember ever feeling as good as this. He glows. Squeezes harder. Feels Heather's damp cheek pressed against his. He whispers into her ear, "I love you." He is released. Employees press in, hands outstretched. There are kisses, handshakes, hugs, expressions of appreciation and good wishes. The president approaches for one last handshake.

John More says, "You're a jerk," out loud, not under his breath as he'd feared, and then strides, chest and chin out, to the parking lot.

This is the completion of his earthquake dream, he supposes. The company and its people have dropped into the chasm. Gone. Forever. But he's survived, hasn't he? He drives to the nearest Chevrolet dealer, dumps the money from his briefcase onto a salesman's desk, and picks out a brilliant red Chevette with air, AM–FM and cassette player. He leaves instructions for the car to be delivered to Betsy, then scribbles a note to be taped to the dashboard.

> *Betsy,*
> *Happy retirement.*
>   *John.*

WHAT MAKES A MAN HAPPY?

I can't say I liked my psychologist. Of course, not having been to one before, I had no real terms of reference. I'm not sure what it was I expected, certainly not a youngish woman, but I went because at that point in my life I didn't know what else to do. Someone had recommended Dr. Max Steinbach. No, I remember now, I *read* his name — her name, as it turned out — in the weekend newspaper. Dr. Steinbach was quoted in an article on how to put the joy back into marriage, a topic I found of particular interest, and I liked what he had to say about the subject. I mean *she* said, though as I indicated, I didn't know that when I made the appointment. About Max being a woman, I mean.

"How can I help you?" Dr. Steinbach asked, after I'd settled into the green velour chair in her tiny office.

I fought to camouflage my discomfort. Doubts about the process had begun to bubble up even when I thought the psychologist was a man, but I'd been determined to see a shrink and had rehearsed what I'd say: that I'd fallen in love with a young woman at the office; that I knew it was wrong and I hadn't told anyone else about it, certainly not the girl, and I had no intention of *doing* anything about it, but I *was* getting tired of the pain and the guilt and hoped an orderly explanation would empower me to untwist these compelling knots in the gut and up in my brain, and to send my dithering heart or soul, or whatever it was, back to my wife, where it obviously belonged. But I couldn't tell that to a slim, short woman whose fair hair was pulled back tightly from her face and tied with a crisp white ribbon. So I said, "I have a weight problem." I don't think I let the surprise show, in my eyes, on my face or through my body language. I'm sure I didn't crack my knuckles or cross and uncross my legs. My ear lobes didn't get tugged, as some people say I have a habit of doing. As far as I can tell, there was no evidence to reveal I'd anticipated a male psychologist.

She repeated my words. "A weight problem."

"Yes. I eat too much. I don't want to, and I decide over and over again to behave myself, not to eat between meals and have extra desserts, but I always do. I'd like to stop, to be able to button up my suit jackets again. I really would."

Max reached for a pad of paper with pale blue lines and began to write. I assumed her name was Maxine, though I didn't have nerve enough to ask. It didn't matter; I wouldn't return to this person. I just had to get the first hour over with, then I was out of there for good. I mean, how do you explain to a young woman about the crazy dreams of an old man? God, how do you explain it to yourself?

Let me clarify the old man statement. Forty-nine isn't old. Not today. I know that. I didn't mean to suggest that it is. So what's my point? Simply that this would've been hard enough to discuss with another man, even one my own age; it was impossible to share with a woman who couldn't have been more than thirty. Probably less. Let's say twenty-eight, the same age as Candy Kalinovski.

The first session wasn't all that bad. Not that it provided any help, but Max never embarrassed me and I was grateful. She asked about Mom and Dad, and how many children were in our family and their ages. Ordinary stuff. Just to put things into perspective, she said. Before we finished the session, Max asked me to keep a diary for her. "Jot down happenings that seem important. Events you have strong feelings about. And if you have dreams, jot them down, too."

Oh sure, I thought, just what I need. Write down *my* dreams. To show to a psychologist. To prove I've lost my marbles and should be locked up. Oh sure. She made an appointment for the following week and I didn't have enough nerve to say no. Not right then, to her face. I thought I'd cancel the appointment before the day arrived. Who knows why I didn't?

Dr. Steinbach realized right away that I wasn't there because of overeating, though the roll around my middle should've made the story believable. She never challenged me about the reasons for my attendance, however, and we had interesting discussions over the weeks on a number of topics: corporate ethics, stress at work, the difficulty of dealing with teenage children, of whom I had three, handfuls all. I was feeling pretty comfortable about the situation, even wondering if maybe I *could* talk about my still simmering love for Candy, when Max made the request.

"I want you to write something for me."

"I can't."

"You said you're a writer."

"No. I said an English teacher told me once that I had a way with words, that I should *consider* being a writer."

"You *want* to be a writer."

"That doesn't *make* me one. I've never written anything. Only business letters, memos."

"Then write something now: a story, an essay."

"What about?"

Maxine smiled. I have to tell you that when Maxine Steinbach smiled, it was easy to forget she wore no make-up and was as austere-looking as her office. I prayed I wouldn't start dreaming about *her*. She said, "Write about what makes a man happy."

The session was over. There wasn't time to argue. While I didn't promise to take on the assignment, to write something, I didn't say I wouldn't. Which is why I'm at this point now, trying to get something down on paper about a subject that seems simple. It's not that easy, though. I've made three starts already and had to throw them all away.

What *does* make a man happy?

It's a clever assignment, don't you think? Max may find out a lot about the inside of me. More than she's learned so far in therapy. So this exercise must be done with care, mustn't show more than I'm prepared to reveal. I mean, there are dark caverns of the mind even *I* haven't seen yet. Know what I mean? Maxine shouldn't arrive there before I do. And then only if it makes sense for her to have a peek, which, in many of my dungeons, I suspect it will not. Would you want a light shone into your dark corners?

I begin reading certain magazines, something I don't usually do, but I need something to kick-start this assignment. I underline a passage from a book review in *Saturday Night*: "The author makes it easy for the reader to suspend belief and, at least for a while, to escape from the humdrum and leave behind the burdens of everyday living." I underline other sentences, too. Later, it startles me to find, in an Alice Munro story in *The Atlantic Monthly*, the question: "Meanwhile, what makes a man happy?" I think, Aha! Now I know where Max got the idea for this exercise. That puts me a step ahead of her. I read the short story a second time, searching for clues. Certain passages get marked with a yellow highlighter, to help me fathom the story. I ask myself what I really understand about the characters, and am disappointed. There must be more to this. Are there symbols I've missed? Have I failed to grasp a layer of insight? Perhaps I'm stupid. My father suggested that when I was a kid. Quite often, as a matter of fact.

Dr. Steinbach had asked me what magazines I read. I'm sure I told her *The Atlantic*, along with *Saturday Night* and a couple of others. I didn't, really, but they were the best names I could think of on the spur of the moment. What was I going to say, that I subscribe to *Playboy*? Maxine is a clever woman. She must have known I'd buy *The Atlantic* and read this particular story; now she expects me to find help in the Munro words. Am I to recognize myself somewhere on these pages? I don't. Is the story supposed to help unravel the covering over self? It doesn't. Fiction is beyond me, it seems. I certainly can't write a story of my own. If I'm unable to understand the respectable lies of another, surely I can't create any useful ones of my own. An essay may be a better form in which to describe what makes a man happy. I'll try that, if I can think of an appropriate topic.

Sex.

Is that what my feelings for Candy are all about? Would the whole thing be resolved by a turbulent roll in the hay? I *have* thought about going to bed with Miss Kalinovski. She's well put together. The fantasy, however, brings no great joy. The truth is that I worry too much about my performance, the age difference, all the things that could go wrong. To be perfectly honest, I'm not one of those men who can dip his pen into any inkwell and write a poem every time. I couldn't make love with a woman who didn't adore me in a powerful, consuming kind of way. To be turned on, I need a partner who can't keep her hands off me, who thinks about me day and night, who cries every morning when I leave her to go to the office. Which pretty well guarantees I'll never be promiscuous, wouldn't you say?

Candy sees me only as another clerk. An old one, losing his hair, blind without bifocals. There's no danger of my having an affair. But let's suppose, for the sake of the essay. Suppose Candy Kalinovski *did* fall in love with me, with that sweeping kind of passion I feel is so important. Would sex make me happy then? Is that what I'm to write for Max?

It can't be. Sex is too fleeting, too transient, too small a part of life to be granted such importance. My wife and I have discussed this, you know. Our honeymoon was hardly over before frequency became an issue. It seems she tired quickly of my constant groping, my apparently insatiable appetite for her. We were making love one morning before breakfast when her irritation finally surfaced. "There are other things we can do together besides this!" she blurted out.

"I realize that," I said, pulling away, shocked by a harsh edge I'd never heard in her voice before. But I hadn't realized, I'm ashamed to admit.

She never actually said I was oversexed, but that was the implication, and I had to agree. Making love was always on my mind in those early days. In my own favour, though, let me point out that I got good at controlling myself, at preventing desire from seeping through my pores, even when she stepped from the shower and danced by me, naked, on the way to the linen closet for a towel. I became quite strong, I'm proud to say. Balanced may be a better word. It was my wife who taught me that life must be balanced. One shouldn't eat too much, drink too much or work too much. And while there's a legitimate place for sex in life, she explained, it's not a large place (unless one needs to make a baby). So one shouldn't write that sex makes a man happy, at least not for more than a very short time, and happiness measured in minutes may not be happiness at all. Anyway, that's not a thought I care to share with Maxine, my psychologist.

One thing that surprises me is how the need to exercise control over my libido hasn't really diminished. They say once you pass forty, sex is over, done with. The truth seems to be that it's never over. At least not in the head, which is where all the trouble begins anyway. But Dr. Steinbach mustn't flush this stuff into the open. Even if she did, I'd tell her that I dream about Candy and me mostly in a non-sexual context. Walking through the park and holding hands. Trite, but nice. What I need. Huddling together beneath an umbrella in a summer shower. Cuddling together in the balcony to watch a good movie. Talking. In my dreams about Candy there's a *lot* of talking. We *walk* and talk, *sit* and talk, *lie* and talk. But there's no sex. Not much of it, anyway. I continue to be in complete control of my baser desires, even in my dreams. So sex isn't the problem. Nor the solution.

But if not sex, what else is there? Wealth? Power? Are these the things to write about? I've never had much of either, but I doubt they're what make a man happy. Wouldn't you agree? The media constantly reports on sad presidents, miserable movie stars, unhappy kings and depressed athletes. Having a mansion or a Mercedes, being able to pay all your bills the moment they arrive, though better than the alternatives, doesn't guarantee good times like so many people seem to think. My dad had a certain amount of power when he was a supervisor at the tire factory, with twelve men reporting to him, plus a female clerk or two, but I don't ever remember thinking he was a happy man. He never played with us kids. He was a walking thunder-storm, bellowing at my mom as well as at my brothers and sisters and me. If he ever told a joke, it wasn't in front of us. There weren't many laughs in our house, even when *we* tried to tell a funny story, real or made up, because he always told us to quit clowning around and finish our chores. When the depression came in the 30s and dad lost his job, along with almost everyone else in the neighbourhood, the gloom and doom others experienced for the first time was normal for us.

I spend my spare time now, and too much time that isn't spare, thinking about this damn essay. Max expects me to arrive tomorrow with a manuscript under my arm. It must help the process without giving too much away. I'm having a terrible time. My efforts say nothing, or they say too much. Apparently there isn't a lot in my life to share. For example, I don't want Dr. Steinbach to know my wife thinks I'm a neatness nut. When I say, "I wish you'd put the cap back on the toothpaste," she snaps back, "Put it on yourself, Felix Unger." There's nothing wrong with neatness, as far as I can see. Don't you agree? How my wife puts up with the clutter that exists in our house is beyond me, and I don't know why she complains when I clean up. There are many reasons for being neat: less chance of an accident, more likely to find something when you want it. My father may have had his faults, but being untidy wasn't one of them. His favourite expression was: "A place for everything, and everything in its place. That's what I always say." When I told my wife what dad always said, she went berserk.

"You're *both* damned compulsives! You know what it is? I'll tell you what this is all about: control! You and your father *both* have to be in control! *All* the time! In *every* little thing!"

My office manager, on the other hand, congratulates me on my neatness. She points out my desk to new employees as a model of organization, so this can't be such a bad attribute. I'd better not write about it for Max, just in case. You see, over the years my wife has been right about an awful lot of things. The truth is she's just as smart as the psychologist. Certainly way above Candy Kalinovski. No doubt about that. So why do I still hanker for this cute, sweet-smelling girl who'll never be a rocket scientist? And hardly knows I even exist? Damned if I know. But that's why I'm seeing Max, and why I'm trying to write about what makes a man happy. *This* man, anyway, though I may not be that much different from other men. I hope not. In this regard, I prefer to be normal.

There must be more to this Alice Munro story than I've been able to figure out. Maxine had a reason for directing me to it. I read this rather long piece of fiction again. I'm not a fast reader, so it takes me a while to get through it, and this time something different happens. I don't hear our clock ticking, the way I usually do. I'm not conscious that the room is cold. I don't feel hungry. I don't worry about Candy or Max or my wife or the essay or how the hell I'm going to make it through the rest of my life. Amazing. I'm in Scotland with Hazel and

Antoinette and Dudley Brown, deciding which of them I like and dislike. Jack is at the top of my dislike list. I stop, consider, wonder. Maybe I'm on to something. Munro has allowed me to lift off from this world, made me forget that her story is just something made up, a figment of her imagination. Her words have managed to transport me out of myself, away from all the old injuries that I'll carry through time, unhealed.

Finally, I set the magazine aside and take up my pen. I write: "What makes a man happy?"

I stop to think about this some more. What's just happened to me, I mean. I talk to myself, the way most of us do when we're troubled about something. Is Candy my Alice Munro? Because it seems so silly when I say it out loud, I don't write it down. Nor can I find the right words to describe the joy of not-real things, not in such a way I can be sure Max will buy it without a lot more probing, which I don't want her to do, so I come up with some generalities about magic and the suspension of belief systems. I write them down. One more sentence is needed to finish the essay so I return to the passages I've highlighted in the magazines. I find exactly what I need to finish my essay.

"The secret is in the acuity of the act of invention."

I don't kid myself, mind you. I know Dr. Steinbach will recognize that I borrowed the line from a book review. The point is, she'll understand what it means, especially in our context, even if I'm not sure myself. Exactly. It sounds good though, wouldn't you say? Max will be damn proud of me.

I hope.

I AM

I admit it, I don't know much about head-stuff: but then I never had the chance to study psychology. My dad's dead now but I remember he never had much use for any of those fancy behaviourial theories anyway.

"Life's only common sense," he announced when I was about 15. We were on a camping trip near Meadow Lake: he and I and our Pastor, and most of the Young Disciples of Christ teen group from our church in Regina. The fire crackled. The sing-song ended and while the guys waited for a ghost story they somehow got talking about kooks and shrinks. "We don't need no Freud or Jung or Schopenhauer to sort out our lives," my dad said with authority. I could see he was pleased we paid attention. "All we got to do is the common sense stuff, like going to church every Sunday, reading the Bible every day, and doing unto others as we'd have them do unto us."

Just because I still don't know about head-stuff doesn't mean I don't think about it, though. For example, I've always believed I had a decent amount of humility down in me somewhere, and that it must be a good thing to have, because as far back as I can remember it's been natural for me not to think overly much of myself. Whenever my dad asked how come I hadn't got better marks on some school exam — I found him tough to please, from kindergarten all the way up to high school — my answer always was, "I guess I'm just kind of stupid." I don't think I truly believed I was stupid, not *dumb* stupid, it was just an easy answer that always seemed to be good enough. I don't remember getting any arguments about it.

I also recall my mother asking me — I was 17 — how come I didn't have a girl friend, and I replied, "I don't know, Ma. I guess I'm so ugly no girl wants to go out with me, that's all."

"Now Bryan," she chided, "don't you get yourself in no dither. There's more important things in life than being handsome, you know, like for instance looking after that precious soul Jesus gave you. Anyway, when the right girl comes along she won't care none about your looks."

Mom was right about the girl, as she seemed to be about most things. Melanie wasn't put off by my sharp-featured face or my flaming red hair or my horrid freckles. I don't know why she settled for me — she's a pretty woman, actually, who could have done much better for herself — but I'm thankful. She's been a good wife and mother to our children. There's no doubt I've done better than I deserve.

Melanie never studied psychology, either. Her folks were still on welfare at the time she should have gone on to the halls of higher learning, and she had to quit school and get a job. She's interested in that sort of thing, though, and often buys *Psychology Today* and also reads articles in *Reader's Digest*. We were still only going together when Mel first said to me, "I wish you'd stop putting yourself down, Bryan."

I was pleased about that. It made me feel good to have someone protest and occasionally offer assurances that I wasn't ugly or stupid or sometimes maybe even mental. I never stopped the put-downs, though — I couldn't, it seems — and I came to depend on Mel sticking up for me whenever I tried to tear myself apart. I won't say that's what attracted me to her, but it is fair to say it was important.

One day she said, "I don't think you have a very good sense of self-esteem, Bryan."

"What does that mean?" I thought I knew, but I wasn't a hundred percent sure and didn't want to display my ignorance, just in case.

"You don't seem to like yourself very much."

That I clearly understood. "I suppose so," I agreed, "but then what's to like?" I had hoped for a good answer, perhaps even a long answer, but the phone rang and after that I guess Mel forgot.

I'm an advertising copywriter now at a Toronto radio station. Melanie says I'm good with words and that I should be writing plays or a novel or something, and I would like to do that, but the truth is I'm just a hack. A pretty good hack probably, because I do know how to sell stuff with words, but just a hack. There's no point in kidding yourself about an important thing like talent. I don't have a lot; not like Saul MacCoy, for example. Now *there's* a good writer.

I remember the time I was interviewing applicants for our second copywriter's position. Most of the candidates had been women: young, recent graduates of one area school or another, all eager to become part of the show biz world of broadcasting. A few admitted to wanting the job only for its weekly paycheque. Some explained confidently — they had lots of self-esteem is my guess — that this would be only a stop on the way to fame as a Hollywood screen writer or a New York author of mainstream novels. One desperate girl crossed a marvellous pair of long legs, hiked her skirt a couple of inches, and hinted huskily that her gratitude, if she was selected, would know no bounds.

Anyway, my choice for the job that day was the next person I saw: Saul MacCoy. He hadn't arrived at my office in a three-piece suit and a silk tie as so many of the male applicants had done. Nor had he carried a folder bulging with unpublished manuscripts to display his creativity. "I'm a writer," Saul had announced simply, his voice gentle and elegant, "and I need a job." There was the hint of a British accent, matching his tweed trousers and prickly-looking wool sweater, and as we talked I knew lady-long-legs would have to be grateful elsewhere. Saul was clear-eyed and intelligent. I knew he was a writer. A *real* writer, not a hack like me, and that's what the radio station, and me too, needed just then.

From the beginning the man was a model employee: punctual, dependable, and hard-working. I was irritated at first because he chose to ignore every negative comment I made about myself. "You're a better writer than me," I told him at the beginning of his second month on the job. Saul just rolled a sheet of paper into his typewriter and set the keys to clattering.

As our relationship developed we became sounding boards for each other's work. One day Saul said, "If the sales department brings me one more used-car dealer I'll puke."

"Whatcha got now?" I asked.

"Some Ford dealer up in Newmarket. Brad Miller. I've already written *five* car commercials today, for Christ's sake."

"Newmarket? Why not hang your copy on that? You know: miles from the high-priced Toronto real estate — lower overhead for Brad Miller means lower car prices for you — that sort of thing."

Saul eased his lanky frame free of the chair and sauntered to the window overlooking Yonge Street. He gazed down at the bumper-to-bumper traffic, his slender fingers carefully interwoven behind his back. The man had grace. Finally he said, "Sure. I'll create a personality for the guy, make him a hick, call him Farmer Brad. I'll use Don Messer fiddle music to open and close."

I was uncomfortable. "The client might not like being called a farmer. Your idea's good, though. How about *Country* Brad?"

It worked. Country Gentleman Brad Miller sold more cars in the next six months than he had in the previous twelve. Saul and I worked together a lot after that and became, in the hackneyed words of our advertising sales manager, "a dynamite duo." We struggled to keep ourselves from going crazy, from getting bogged down in the usual ruts. We discovered we could create comedy: skits that masqueraded as commercials. When Nikita Khrushchev backed down and removed the Soviet missiles from Cuba as President Kennedy demanded, the next day we had an appliance dealer with a Russian accent agree to remove offensively high price tags from his washing machines.

I don't know who was more temperamental, MacCoy or me. When our mood swings counter-balanced, life in the copy department was fine. Between the writing of meat market commercials and discount ladies wear spots, we discussed the intricacies of novel writing: plotting, characterization, the use of symbols, and the differences between short and long fiction. But when we arrived together at the bottom of a down cycle, as we sometimes did, it was impossible for us even to speak to one another.

We learned to cope by invoking an unspoken agreement that one of us would leave the radio station. Though it was possible to get the information required from sponsors over the telephone, we chose on those difficult days to visit our clients in person: Saul one day, I the next. Our advertisers loved the attention. Our successes multiplied. Our respect for each other grew. It was more than that, I think: we liked each other.

It didn't seem unusual when Saul called me at home one night just as I was finishing supper. "I need to see you, Bryan," MacCoy said. "Tonight."

Melanie didn't mind and I arranged to meet Saul in front of the radio station in half an hour. He'd asked that we go for a drive. He didn't speak as he slid onto the front seat of my blue Chevrolet: he didn't have to. He'd been in a dour mood since nine that morning. My own morale had been good but I'd been unable to lift his spirits, to get him giggling again, no matter how hard I tried. I drove away silently, wondering what the problem was, wondering how my clever father — the man who'd once won an award for outstanding service to the citizens of Regina — would have handled a situation like this, wondering what words I might call forth to help. I'm not good at this sort of thing. I knew Saul had sent his manuscript to a publisher some months ago. What would I say if it had been rejected? Perhaps the job was his problem, and I should offer to rearrange the work, taking on some of his most hated accounts myself. He'd done that for me six months earlier.

It didn't take long to reach a country road. We'd been together for 30 minutes and I was becoming conscious of his spicy after-shave — that was a surprise because I'd never noticed it at the office — when Saul spoke for the first time. "Can we stop here?"

I pulled onto the shoulder of the gravel road and we got out of the car. "Want to go for a walk?"

He nodded.

We scrambled over a split-rail fence and hiked toward a heavily-treed area. Fall's finery was spread on the ground like a coat of many colours, covering tree roots as if to hold in what remained of summer's warmth. It was a perfect evening: windless, noiseless, and without the mosquitoes that had made summer evenings miserable only a few weeks earlier. The aroma of the woods and the feel of leaves underfoot called up, for me, memories of another Young Disciples camping trip.

I'd been 9. I was thinking about the nudist magazine one of the guys had brought, and my reaction to seeing a naked woman for the first time, when Saul stopped. We were deep in the forest.

"I like this," he said, his gentle voice down-soft.

"Me too." I waited for him to explain why he'd asked for this meeting.

"And I like you, too."

That pleased me. "You know I think of *you* as a good friend."

"Let's take off our clothes," my co-worker suggested. "We'll both feel more comfortable and relaxed."

I couldn't respond. It was as though I'd been punched in the windpipe. I watched, speechless, as he undid the buttons of his cotton shirt, then let it drop to the leaf-padded earth. His chest was smooth and a pale pink. Next came his shoes and socks. Saul's feet were small and perfectly shaped: not calloused like mine. His boxer shorts came down at the same time as his cords and he stood before me naked. He said, "Come on, my friend. Join me." He sat down, his back pressed against the rugged bark of a giant maple, and smiled up at me. I'd never seen Saul MacCoy look as tranquil as he did at that moment. It was as if he'd found the *peace that passeth all understanding* that my father kept reading about in the Bible.

I opened my mouth but nothing came out. My face was hot and red. I swivelled and raced — it was as if a grizzly was after me — all the way back to the Chevrolet. My heart pounded. My lungs were out of air. The pieces of my mind whirled crazily, as though they'd been dropped into a food processor. What was wrong with me that I'd attracted this man? Was it the high-pitched voice I'd hated all my life? Or was there a deficiency in my character that caused him to believe I was gay? What had I said? And why hadn't I been smart enough to perceive his sexual preference? I'd known he lived with another man but had naively assumed his room-mate was simply a sharer of expenses and chores.

What should I do now? I couldn't drive off and leave the man alone in the country, could I? If my father was still alive, what would he say about this? What would he think of me now?

My father: the man who'd been so much more intelligent than I, so worldly-wise, so highly regarded at City Hall where he'd worked as the municipal clerk for more than 20 years. My father: the man whom I'd never been able to please. I'd fallen far short of his expectations, right from the beginning.

The man next door had been over for a beer. I was supposed to be in bed, asleep, but I'd gotten up for a glass of water. I heard my dad say, "You're lucky your kid's a good athlete. Bryan is so clumsy he can hardly walk without falling down. I always hoped for a son who'd be good at some sport. Hockey woulda been my choice, or baseball. Just my luck, though: the only boy I get turns out to be a klutz."

As I sat behind the wheel of my Chevy, listening to a bluebottle buzz and bang against the windshield, smelling the fields of cut grain, knowing now I could not, would not leave until Saul came back to the car, I realized I *had* been able to please my father, in one way at least. The knowledge had been there all the time, deep down in the well, but I had never allowed myself to bring up the bucket.

Refocusing on the image of a nude Saul MacCoy, lean, long out of the sand-coloured pubic hair, I saw again my father doffing his clothes in my bedroom. I was six, seven at most, and I didn't understand why his garments were coming off, why his penis was erect, why he was climbing into my bed. I followed his directions, embarrassed, did what I was told to do, was frightened beyond words by his moaning and threshing. I never understood how this came to be a Sunday morning ritual, completed early enough that it never interfered with our going to church together, or how my mother and sisters never heard, never questioned, never came to my room next door to see what was happening.

I heard a sound: distant thunder growing rapidly louder, and looked in the rear-view mirror to see a pick-up truck hurtling down the country road with a swirling cloud of gravel dust. I glanced nervously toward the woods. When I'd made the decision to wait for Saul I'd assumed he'd get dressed before returning to the car. What would I do if he strolled out of the forest still naked? What if someone should come by and see a nude man climbing in beside me? I'd be labelled a queer. Melanie might disown me.

Maybe I am gay.

My father began to masturbate me shortly after his first visit. I didn't say no. I liked it, I guess, though I always suffocated in my guilt afterwards. It wasn't until my 16th birthday that I put an end to it. It had been simple enough to do when I finally made up my mind. I made sure I was fully dressed when he came into my room. I looked up from my desk and announced, "It's over. If you don't leave me alone, I'll write a letter to the mayor. Tell him everything we've ever done: the sex, the dirty magazines, everything."

"You're a piece of shit," my father said, but he never came back to my room.

When Saul arrived at the car, about the same time as the pick-up blasted past, spewing stones, he was dressed. "Thank you for waiting, Bryan," he whispered. "I appreciate it." Pain was smeared across his face.

I started the Chevrolet. "That's okay." It wasn't what I wanted to say. It was barely adequate just to keep up one end of a conversation, but it was the best I could do.

We were almost back in the city when Saul said, "I'll give you my resignation in the morning."

"I don't want it. It's not necessary."

"I can't stay."

"Of course you can. I don't want to lose you. What happened out there, my running away like a stupid kid, is my fault, not yours. I can't explain it now, but you don't have to leave."

He placed his hand on mine. It was the firm touch of a good friend, not a lover. "I heard from the publisher today, Bryan," he explained. "He bought my novel. I'm sorry to leave you, but he wants me to get started on my next book. I need to get to work on it."

I parked in front of the radio station. "Congratulations, Saul MacCoy. I'm happy for you," I said, meaning it. Only a little envious. "And good luck."

He got out, closed the door, then leaned down to look at me through the window frame one last time. I wondered why I'd never noticed before that Saul's eyes were the same shade of chestnut brown as my father's. He said, "I'll miss you, Bryan. You're a good man." Then he was gone.

I looked at myself in the mirror for a minute, then nodded. I wheeled the Chevrolet out to merge with the traffic on Yonge Street.

CLOUD HERDING

The storm clouds assemble on this sweltering summer day. The laundry should come in now but I let Charles' shirts and the children's jeans hang dankly in the still air. I rock on the back porch, satisfied with the accuracy of my morning horoscope, "Watch out for dark anger in high places." I find the relationship between the heavens and the affairs of mankind fascinating; Charles insists it's mystical mumbo jumbo. If father were alive, he'd also think it strange that his little girl has become a believer in telekinesis, extra-sensory perception and clairvoyance. I was never interested in such things before I got married. Back then I always maintained that *Twilight Zone* was for the immature. *Star Trek* bored me.

The first gust of wind attacks the drops of sweat beading on my neighbour's forehead as he leans on his lawnmower. A screen door slams. The shirts are flapping now, the jeans slapping. I let them boogie. Bolts of lightning precede fat rain drops. Approaching thunder obliterates the hum of the kitchen fan. It's too late to worry about getting the clothes in. I manage only to get the upstairs windows closed before the downpour begins.

Is it storming at the summer camp? I hope the girls haven't been caught out in a canoe. In the almost-dark of the bruised sky I settle back into my rocker. Water splatters through the wood rails onto my bare legs, and I force them forward for more. Who is washing my feet, gently working the cool, sweet-smelling rain between my tired toes? A spirit from the past, a former inhabitant of this century-old house? It's a woman; no man was ever so gentle. I hope she approves of the manner in which I maintain her mansion. Does she understand my loneliness?

I'd like to send her to search for Papa. His name is Alex Gizikis," I want to tell her, "a handsome, dark-haired Greek. He once owned a small restaurant at the corner of Dundas and George in Toronto. He's a man who was never daunted by the trials of existence, not like me, and I need to talk to him. Tell him it's his daughter, Mary Ann, the one who danced on his counter for nickels when she was four. He'll remember."

The storm ends. The air is cool, wet and clean. I smell the after-effects of the lightning, shattered ozone mixed with rain on the roses. Papa had his heart attack and took up residence in a tree outside my bedroom window when I was eleven. We talked regularly after that, Papa and I, and he was a great comfort until I was fourteen. "Mamma won't let me date Johnny Antonio," I told him once. "She says I'm too young."

"It's not that you're so young," Papa replied, "but that the Antonio boy is not good enough for my little girl. Wait: a good Greek will call. Then you'll date."

I told him how Mamma was always at me. "Sit up straight. Hold your fork in the other hand. Pull down your skirt. When I tell you to do something, Mary Ann Gizikis, I expect you to do it."

"Don't I know," Papa sighed. "I love Mamma almost as much as I love you, but she does the same to me."

The day the workmen came to cut down the tree — it was old and Mamma said it might come down in a storm — I kicked up an awful fuss. I screeched, tossed dishes, stomped to my room and refused to come out. A snarling chain saw ignored my threat never to eat again and ripped the tree down. I heard it crash; smelled the damp, woody sawdust. After that, Papa never talked to me again.

A good Greek did not call, either. I was 17 when Charles Krasinski came around. He was Polish, not Greek, quite handsome and much taller than I. He had four sisters and I went to school with Ginny, the youngest. I also knew his father, Kasimierz, the man who sold us our meat. He was the only man I knew who worked as hard as Papa. He liked me, always cut me a slice of kielbasa and asked about Mamma. I wished Mrs. Krasinski would go to heaven so Kasimierz could become my father.

89

After the rain, the mosquitoes arrive. They hover over my legs, buzz around my ears. It's time to try my mind-over-matter meditation technique. It gets rid of arthritic pain. When my leg aches I close my eyes, inhale deeply, then breathe out slowly and force the ache down my leg, along my foot and out through my toes. The hurt disperses into the air. I close my eyes and inhale; imagine a shield around my body emitting such a powerful force-field the insects will be driven away. The mosquitoes draw blood and I conclude that insects are immune to meditation. I go inside.

It's time to start supper. Chuck will be home soon and, if I've interpreted his horoscope correctly, he won't want to be kept waiting. He's often cranky after a tough day at the office. He worked hard to become a vice president and deserves all the respect that goes with such a position, but sometimes he makes me feel like an employee. This doesn't please me. His secretary got bombed at the Christmas party last year and told me Charles was a dictator. She called him blunt and abrasive, a Mafia godfather. According to her, he expects everyone on earth to work as much as he does — twelve hours a day, seven days a week. A typical Leo.

There isn't much to complain about, however. Our houses have grown bigger, if not newer. The one we live in now is the best yet; it has character. I call it our castle because of the two-storey protrusion of curved windows at the front. Our foyer could almost accommodate a sit-down dinner. Maybe I am complaining. The smaller houses were fine. I assume we moved to show his success to the world, but maybe he thinks this is what *I* want.

We don't talk much. I can get my ESP going on him sometimes. Silently I'll say, "You want to go to bed." I focus my mind on our antique four-poster and say the words: "Bed, bed, bed; you want to go to bed." It works 50 percent of the time. "You are hungry," gets better results and, "You want a drink," gets through eight times out of ten. "Talk to me," seldom works. I don't think it's because he doesn't get the ESP message, just that he's stubborn. Perhaps he's ashamed of me because I was born on my mother's dining room table in the flat over Papa's restaurant. Maybe not. I don't think I ever told him.

TV dinners will be good enough tonight. It's too hot to cook. I might have prepared crabmeat salad on a lettuce raft and sliced some tomatoes, but there wasn't time to go shopping. I had to do the washing. I pop the dinners into the microwave and wonder why Chuck bought such a miraculous machine when he won't discuss air-conditioning. The BMW slides into the driveway. I slosh Chivas over ice cubes in Chuck's favourite glass, aware this isn't extra sensory perception. We've gone through this routine for ten years.

"Hi hon, how was your day?"

"Tough."

"I figured. Here's your scotch."

"Thanks. How was your day?"

"Boring."

"Good. I'm going upstairs to change."

The way I heard it, his older sisters spoiled him rotten. They picked up his clothes, made his bed, helped him with school work. They had a built-in radar for spotting his hurts: the girl who turned down his invitation to the dance, the part in a school play that went to someone else. They comforted him, mothered him, selected his girlfriends and told him his own choices weren't the right type for him. Before a date they'd say, "Are you sure you want to wear that?" and he'd go back and change. I got all this from Ginny. She talked them into recommending me. I was glad then; now I'm not sure.

We sit in the dining room. Charles says nothing about the TV dinners. Leo the Lion doesn't squander emotion on anything as mundane as food. He holds out his glass. I pour more. More for me, too. I remember when we had a business party and he introduced me to the president of some company. "This is my wife, Mary Ann," he said, one hand on my shoulder. "An amazing woman. Looks after my needs, and the children's, wonderfully well." I only find out what he thinks when he talks to someone else. "Oh, Mary Ann's very bright," he told another man. "She just stays in the background because I need someone who doesn't compete."

When we went to bed I asked, "Why don't you ever talk to me?"

"What?"

"Why don't you talk to me?"

"I'm talking to you now, aren't I?"

"You never told me you think I'm bright."

"Didn't I?"

I propped myself up on one arm. "How would I compete with you?"

"What?"

"You said you need someone who won't compete. So, how would I?"

"Go to sleep," Chuck said. "It was only small talk."

That's when I began reading about how to change brain-wave patterns. I studied psychic force fields. Commercial magic holds no interest for me; there's too much illusion already. Religion has no appeal, either. Remember the mass suicide at Jonestown? I bought a deck of Tarot cards, and a book about dreams, and I went to the library to find out about the Society for Psychic Research, but I didn't tell Chuck. He wouldn't understand. Mother says loneliness is preferable to an empty togetherness. Perhaps she's right.

I pour more scotch and accept his grunt as thanks. The heat is stifling. I wonder if I dare mention air-conditioning again. I sip and say, "It's bad enough you don't talk to me; you don't listen, either."

"Of course I listen."

"Do you remember asking how my day was?"

Charles sighs. "Of course."

"And do you remember my answer?"

"You said fine, like always."

"No. I told the truth; I said my day was boring."

"Boring?"

"Boring."

"I'm sorry," he says. He gets up from the table, takes his glass and goes to the front room to watch the news. I'm angry; perspiring and angry. A cool puff of air brushes my right cheek, sending shivers down my spine. It's the lady of the house, the spirit who washed my feet in the storm, and she is telling me something. What? Has she found Papa? Does she have a message from him? When I step toward the kitchen to do the dishes, the air puff brushes my other cheek. She wants me to follow Charles, directs me into the living room, then over to the box spewing world news. I reach down and shut the television off. Chuck's eyebrows rise like lift-bridges. Aries I, impulsive, exult. I am gently blown to his chair. Reaching for his hand, I pull him to his feet.

"What the hell are you doing?"

"Shh," I say, listening for I know not what, waiting for another breath. We each have a glass in one hand, each other in the other. Guided, I lead him to the garden. We sink into side-by-side chaise lounges and lie there, staring up. I smell the grass, the damp soil of the flower beds, the roses. And Charles' cologne. It surely hasn't lasted since he shaved this morning. Did he apply more when he changed? If he thinks that's all it will take to get me in the mood, he can forget it.

The air is still. If the lady of the house is present, she leaves us on our own. Sounds paint summer pictures: a cricket, an ice cream bell, the distant cry of a baby. Chuck stares at the summer sky, a brilliant blue spotted with cotton clouds. "Have you ever tried cloud herding?" he asks. His voice is quiet, resonant.

I don't know what he's talking about. "No."

"See that wispy cloud up there, the one shaped like a face with a jolly round nose?"

"I see it."

"What we do is concentrate and see if we can coax it toward us."

The lady of the house hasn't left us, I conclude. She has edged her way into Chuck's heart, forcing out the Leo creativity held in check for so long. I focus upward and say to myself, *Come over here, little cloud. Come on, come on.* The silliness I first felt drains away. I don't know how long it takes but the face with the jolly nose scuds across the sky.

"Great," Charles says. "That's really good. Now let's try to keep it overhead while we herd more clouds over. Let's see how big a patch the two of us can make."

I don't know if our cloud herding is telekinesis or coincidence, and I don't care. A brief caress of coolness on my forehead prompts me to say a silent thank you.